HEAD OF STEAM

More Men of Steam Stories
by

RAYMOND FLINT

SANTONA PUBLICATIONS
HULL
1995

Cover design
from an Original Water Colour

THE POWER HOUSE
CASTLEBROUGH LOCOMOTIVE SHED
by
Adrian P Thompson
Water Colour Artist (Hull)

HEAD OF STEAM

First Published 1995
Reprinted   1998

British Library Cataloguing-in-Publication data.

A catalogue record for this book is available from the British Library.

Copyright © 1995 by Raymond Flint.

First published in 1995 by Santona Publications, 3 Lawsons Close,
Hull. HU6 7UW.

Printed and bound by FISK PRINTERS, HULL.

ISBN 0 950796 0 2 6

Also by the same author
The People's Scenario 1982
The March of the History Animal 1985
Men of Steam 1994

The Spirit of Santona

Onward to the horizon

SANTONA PUBLICATIONS
HULL

DEDICATED TO JOAN
my wife of forty-five years
without whom this
book would have never been written and
whose response when I was diagnosed
PARKINSONS DISEASE
was
"We'll have to think of it as just another adventure"

ACKNOWLEDGEMENT

"When I travel with another, I travel with a teacher," words of wisdom credited to Confucius, the ancient Chinese philosopher of 2,500 years ago. How appropriate to all of us.

There have been many travelling companions in my life whose association has enriched and instructed me. The opportunity now presents itself for me to acknowledge their valuable contribution to my life and to the treasure chest of human experience. Who are they?

Sorrow, fear, pity, and bitterness are examples of the emotions which assault our spirits when misfortune or illness besets us. 'How to cope?' is the question that arises with greatest urgency. There is no single answer, only the courageous examples of those who have gone before: like Roy Castle, the Marti Caine, Professor Stephen Hawking, author of 'A Brief History of Time', and countless others. These are our travelling companions who are our teachers.

But of those on my journey not all are high flyers, they are mostly the ordinary man, woman or child; the neighbour whose struggle with eternal pain and mental anguish is an inspiration, the child with cruel disability, and those who face death which by their example give us hope and strength. But all are survivors, role models and the true heroes of the human race; living evidence of human resilience and versatility. They all have one feature in common, a determination to pursue the positive and get on with the joy of life despite the pain and difficulty.

The Parkinsons Disease Society of the United Kingdom gave me such an opportunity to travel with rich teachers and witness examples of dogged determination in the face of increasing adversity. Without their example I would not have decided to be active within their ranks and continue to write. Rather I would have faced the prospect of Parkinsons Disease with timidity and an infinite measure of fear. They and their Society are very important, indeed indispensable, to those who need them. They became my companions on my new journey, and amongst them I found many worthy teachers .

So often have I witnessed the love and care that there is in this world of disability that it has inspired me to believe that there is a basic human goodness that will survive the horrors of the human jungle. I know this from the fruitful years that I spent teaching disabled students in college; I know of it from the voluntary sector with its selfless voluntary workers whose only returns are the care of those whom they serve; I know of it from the parents who, without complaint, give their lives to disabled offspring; I know it from the married partners who modify their lives and ambitions to include a disabled spouse.

Such were my teachers as I travelled with them on a new journey, such do I acknowledge.

I must record also that without the encouragement and faith of my family this book would never have been completed and published. It is part their creation as well as my own.

Ray Flint Nov 1995

PREFACE

'Head of Steam' is the consecutive volume to 'Men of Steam'. As with its predecessor, it illustrates the lives of the railwaymen in Yorkshire during the steam age and brings to life the situations which made up their experiences. I hope what I write does justice to that rugged body of men, women and boys that kept a million wheels rolling on un-ending railway tracks in the 1940's.

Surviving steam locomen and railwaymen from that age think of it as the 'heroic age' when muscle and brawn were the real motive powers behind steam and rail. There had to be steam in the blood. There were no electric switches or electric lights, no speedometers, few places to eat in comfort and often no piped water, toilets, washing or sleeping facilities.

Heavy signal levers had to be manhandled all day in thousands of cabins. Locomotive reversing screws and levers had to be re-positioned tirelessly. Resistant steam regulators had to be pulled open or closed countless times in the working day. Long lengths of steel rails had to be lifted by hand from or to wagons and rail beds. The constant coupling and uncoupling of thousands of wagons each day: the list is endless but illustrative of the hard work of the steam age.

I hope to play a part in recalling that heroic age to our consciousness. I hope also to entertain the reader and to promote an awareness of steam railway heritage in Yorkshire.

If I am spared the ravages of time I hope to produce a further sequel, or even sequels but that is at the mercy of forces over which I, like you, have no power. In the meantime I commend this volume to you and wish you an enjoyable read, indeed, an enjoyable experience on the steam railways of Yorkshire in the 1940's.

Ray Flint 1995

HEAD OF STEAM

CONTENTS

1
DANGER HIGH EXPLOSIVE

Why should Jingo need to be seen by the railway bobby? Joe wished he knew, he'd only heard part of Bill Frobisher's message to Jingo in the messroom. "When you get back this afternoon Franker wants to see you. Arranging for Maurice Wells to ask you questions about the burglary at Gallows."

Joe was too tired to express his curiosity to Jingo. The journey from Castlebrough to Church Fenton on the old D20 loco with its double-headed string of 85 empty coal wagons and his overpowering early morning fatigue kept him quiet. The hard frost, the hedgerows, gutters full of dirty frozen snow; the dark misty morning, his battered face, and being called out early for this special run, added up to an uncomfortable, tiresome experience for him.

"Goin' to be all bloody day again," cursed Jingo to no one in particular, almost as though he was talking through his long teeth to himself. "All the bloody boards are on at Fenton. Signalman's on his arse again."

Simpson, the driver on the J27 leading engine started to apply the joint vacuum brake that operated the linked braking system on the two engines. The two engine whistles blasted loud and long to convey irritation to the Church Fenton signalman. The long string of loose coupled wagons jostled and buffeted as they protested noisily against the sudden braking.

"That'll knock Matt off his seat mate," said Joe, referring to the train's guard.

"Somebody's got to wake the bugger up. If I'd had the brake handle instead of Simpson, he'd be stuck to the end wall of his brake van now like a bloody fly on fly paper." Already the time was 10am and they were just completing the outward journey to Gascoigne Wood, the vast marshalling yard for the coal wagons of West Yorkshire collieries.

"He's pulling off now. His advance is off, George." Joe used Jingo's real name rather than his nickname; the name that had stuck since George earned it from his continuous agitation against the 'threat' from the Yellow Peril.

"They'll flood Britain if we don't keep 'em out and make 'em stop in China," Jingo would say. "Even if a battalion of Guards has to occupy China and Japan to subdue them."

"Jingoistic bastard," Bloomer the shed's most vocal and

argumentative communist would respond.

"Britons never, never, shall be slaves. Rule Britannia." George Johnson would reply.

"Jingoistic bastard."

"The sun never sets on the British Empire. One-sixth of the world won for you by old soldiers like me."

"Jingoistic bastard. We're goin' to alter that."

George Johnson didn't mind the nickname that he'd earned, there were plenty of Georges on the railways but only one 'Jingo'. Simpson's J27 sounded its whistle twice in acknowledgement of the path that was opening up in front of them. The vacuum ejector exhaust whined away at the chimney top as the brakes on the two engines were released. Jingo, forever purging to be off, whipped open his steam regulator and made his engine roar at the chimney top.

"Get yer head in kiddo. Don't want to close yer other eye with a hot cinder from the chimney."

Joe withdrew from Jingo's side. He agreed, not wanting to have his right eye closed like his left. His cheek and lips were likewise swollen. The injuries had prompted remarks from other railwaymen that he shouldn't be at work. He'd told Jingo, Simpson and Johnny, and indeed all who would listen that morning at 5am in the messroom at Castlebrough, how he'd fought the feared Guy Reynolds, professional boxer, in the ring at the Boys' Club down North Street and come off a very good second best. Joe's account was somewhat at variance with reality.

Boxing ambitions had been inspired by his readings about Joe Louis, Tommy Farr, Carnera and other giants of the square ring with canvas covered boards. There was no example of pugilism in the Wade family or the Peace family, neither had Joe excelled in any sport. Fighting at school was an activity he'd strove energetically to avoid, but he still got picked on by school toughs and involved in painful bruising encounters.

Joe was a peace loving chap with a suppressed Christian love for his fellows, that's how he saw himself but he wasn't a pacifist. It followed that he must be able to defend himself from his less Christian fellows. The rough sport of the twenty or so teenage engine cleaners at Castlebrough turned him to the self-defensive arts. The torment and battering he and other unfortunates experienced in the messroom, the sand hole, or the 'prehistoric' communal water closet, with its three 'cheek by jowl' holes in the common wooden seat, provided the justification for his evenings spent at the Boys' Boxing Club.

With 8oz gloves swinging from his shoulder, Joe would saunter importantly down Hastings Road towards the bus and the club. Was he giving notice to threatening youths? Or creating an image for predatory females? His Father's boastful remark to a quarrelsome work mate, "I've got a lad that'll knock the shit out of you," sounded warning bells for Joe but he still pressed on.

Whatever it was that directed him towards such aggressive practices, he didn't know, but he was bent on a glittering career in the ring. Last night was just an early landmark on what was going to be a chequered career. He'd landed on a 'black' square he consoled himself. Today he was wearing battle scars in the shape of a nearly closed black left eye and a swollen cheek and lip.

"Bin 'ere before kid?" Jingo broke in.

"Few times," returned Joe, "know we're nearly there. Know we won't get back very early. Never do. Sixteen hour day last time I worked this train!"

Jim Simpson, on the front engine was whistling and applying the brakes on the two engines as the long train snaked through Sherburn-in-Elmet towards the marshalling yard that lined both sides of the main line.

"We ain't goner get home afore dark today. Expect a long day," responded Jingo.

A bearded shunter, with shunting pole in hand, jumped on Jingo's engine step as they slowly entered the yard. "You're laid for number seven road. Go right down till you're clear in at the back end. I'll signal you to stop from the other side." He climbed into the cab. "You'll have to go well down 'cos seven road's too short to get all this lot in." He was addressing Jingo. "I've told the other driver to leave the braking to you. When yuh stop he'll loose off and go over the other side of the yard for turning." The shunter passed over to Joe's side to give him some instructions and made to leave the cab. "I'm going to drop off now son and give you a signal from this side to stop when we're clear in. When your mate halts her, you loose off just clear so that he can go forward and then back the front-half of the train into Singleton's sidings. Brake a couple of wagons with a brake stick each time you loose off."

Joe nodded. He was pleased to be able to get off the footplate and run around on the hard frozen ground amongst the wagons. He knew what he had to do, he'd done such manoeuvres before. He dropped from his engine as it rolled past the point where he had to break the train in two and waited for Jingo to heed the shunter's signal to halt. With two wagon handbrakes secured tightly to stop the wagons following them, Jingo moved forward with the section of train for Singleton's. Simpson's detached J27 loco was chugging away in the distance towards the turntable and a short breakfast halt.

"Make sure the points go right over and stay shut before you wave me back." Jingo had cautioned Joe. But there was no need for alarm, as Joe had noted mentally, 'I've done this job thousands of times. What yuh nattering at? You look to your own job and leave me to mine.' Discretion dictated to Joe that such remarks were better left unsaid.

A little black smoke and an acrid sulphur smell drifted past Joe's painful nose as the last wagon in the front section rolled away. An audible crackling and a spitting told him an axle-box on the wagon was overheated and smouldering.

Over the points and backing slowly into Singleton's siding, Joe hung on the side of the first wagon. He gave a thumbs up sign to the shunter who'd guided them in until they stopped and then he fastened down a couple of wagon handbrakes. Curiosity made him examine the hot axle-box on the old privately owned wagon which was labelled 'Stores for Cudworth Motive Power Department'. It was unusual to see a loaded wagon among his train's empty coal wagons. He drifted in the direction of his D20 and Jingo, tired and ready to eat his sandwiches.

"You've been hanging about sitting on your bloody thumbs."

"Not really, George. There was an axle-box burning on the first wagon. I just had a look at it. The 'Carriage the Wagon' lads'll spot it when they examine the train and put it out."

"That's what they're paid for."

Joe took to his fireman's seat. "Are we able to go yet?"

Jingo was looking forwards, "Not until this fellow finishes shunting in front of us. He's got us blocked in."

"Go down and ask him to let us out so's we can get across to the turntable. Tell him I've got to be home for three-thirty for an army medical. They need me for the Second Front."

Wondering why the army should be wanting Jingo, Joe set off towards the working shunting engine that blocked their passage, keeping his eyes open and avoiding the loose wagons which were being shunted at speed into the sidings. Dreaming as he walked, he was only gradually aware that the last running-shunt had derailed a wagon. Their exit from the sidings was now blocked. "This will please Jingo," muttered Joe audibly as he went back to report. "He'll never get back for his medical now."

"They'll have to clear Singleton's from the other end to let us out," said Jingo. The expected irritating blast had not been forthcoming. "Tell yer what. Tek my billycan up to the shunters' cabin, just as we came into the yard, remember?" He noted Joe's nodding assent. "Get me some hot watter on this tea and ask 'em to draw off this load and let us out through Singleton's."

A column of black smoke was wisping up from the Cudworth wagon. 'Funny that it ain't burnt out by now. Should've now the wagon's stopped,' Joe thought as he approached the wagon again. The grease in the axle-box was now burning fiercely, flames were licking the wooden wagon. Heat stung his cheeks as he gave a closer inspection and his sore eye smarted in the smoke. Looking through the crack along the side of the drop-down door, he could see sheeted-goods resting in the end of the wagon. Curiosity inspired him to shin up the wagon side, over the top, and pull the tarpaulin aside. He revealed a consignment of stores to Cudworth Motive Power Department; three bales of cotton waste, two drums of kerosene, bundles of sponge clothes, a barrel of superheat oil, firing shovels and some cardboard cartons. A barrel, which had fallen on its side, leaked kerosene which puddled across the wagon floor to feed the flaming axle-box.

Joe almost fell down the side of the wagon, Jingo's can, luckily, survived in Joe's grasp. The smoke column was thickening and the flames were becoming more intense, the whole wagon was going to be consumed by fire. The urgency of the situation struck through Joe's sluggish exterior and injected him with alarm. He dropped to the ground and his hand fell on a boxvan in the next siding. The heat was scorch was scorching.

Red explosives labels held in the wagon invoice clip alerted him to a new problem. The closed and locked boxvans contained explosives for Church Fenton Air Field. 'DANGER EXPLOSIVES' were the words on grubby stick-on labels. There was more than one wagon. 'Bloody big bang if this lot goes up,' he thought. He tried to pass between the burning wagon and the nearest boxvan; the heat drove him back. A quick thought that they would want to move the burning wagon ran through his mind. He passed between the burning wagon and the rest of the train, and as he did he slipped the three-link coupling off the draw hook. The fire, fed with leaking kerosene, was starting to crackle and roar. A menacing orange and black plume rose skyward. He knew the wagon would have to be moved somehow. Urgency propelled him in the direction of the shunters' cabin.

A slow moving, puffing, 0-6-0 War Department saddle tank shunting engine was rolling down the feeder road towards him as he emerged running from Singleton's siding. The engine accelerated, investigation of the thickening column of black smoke its obvious goal.

Joe waved the white billycan to attract attention as he ran.

"What's up mate?" called the driver from the cab of the shunting engine.

"Wagon axle-box," shouted Joe as the little grey six-wheeled engine began to slow to a halt.

"That all? Mekin a lot of bloody smoke," said the shunter as he eased to one side of the cab steps to let Joe grasp the handrail and join the engine. Joe hauled himself up to the cab level.

"Yeh, but it's set the wagon on fire. The wagon's full of cotton waste and kerosene."

"Better send for a fire engine, Charles," said the driver of the saddle tank to his mate. "It's getting well hold."

"Wagons of explosives in the next road." Joe was breathless and agitated. "Got to get our train moved."

"Give me a run down to the shunter's cabin," Charles instructed urgently. "I'll ring from there."

The driver threw the reversing lever into back position and made the little engine scurry off in the direction of the cabin.

"No. No. The next road's got ammo wagons in it," added Joe excitedly. "I've got to get back to my engine, We can move the train. You can't do it from this end, too blooming hot."

"This do yuh? Charles," the driver addressed his mate as the engine screeched to a halt. "I'll go back up there with this lad and look at the situation." He reversed and made his six-wheeled loco scurry back almost before Charles had dropped away from the cab steps. "What yer say son?" He turned to Joe to pick up the spoken unclear sentence he'd almost heard.

"The next road's got ammo wagons in it?" repeated Joe.

"Which side?"

"Top side of Singleton's road."

"The little stores road, Eh? Where you from, son?"

"Castlebrough. We just came in double-headed with a long string of empties and split 'em. Half in seven and half in Singleton's. It's one of our wagons that's blazing."

"Where's yer engine now?"

"Blocked in on the other end of the empties in Singleton's. A wagon off the road is blocking us in. We can't get out until it's put back on or 'til we can get through Singleton's. I should go down and tell my mate to push it clear." Joe was impatient, he felt that time was being wasted. The driver was bent on his own investigation, he was the one to be held responsible, not this swollen faced kid.

The saddle tank engine rolled up closer to the burning wagon. "She's beginning to burn like hell, now. What yer say's in the wagon?" Joe didn't have time to answer. "Kerosene and cotton waste. Did yer say? No wonder it's burning like 'ell."

They leapt from the engine. "Bloody hot now. We'll never get near enough to hang on and pull it clear." The driver observed the possibilities and dangers of the situation and examined the wagon tickets on the first of the four closed vans. "Some ammo for Church Fenton Airfield."

"Yes. I said so," re-acted Joe impatiently.

Urgency gripped the driver. "Let's get to hell out of it. Don't know what's in them wagons but don't want to be here if they go bang."

The little saddle-tank rolled away with the engine crew and Joe as quickly as the regulator could be whipped open by the alarmed driver. Charles was approaching them at a run from his mission to call the firefighters. The now heavy column of black smoke reaching into the sky was sending its message out to railmen all over the marshalling yard. The little engine halted when Charles was aboard and he was given a report of the situation in Singleton's siding.

"I'll go and get all through traffic on the mainlines stopped. If that lot's going up, don't know where it will land when it comes down." Charles was off the engine and galloping towards Milford signal cabin.

"Mate." Joe addressed himself to the driver on the shunting engine. "I'm going back to my mate Jingo. Got to tell him the score. He might be looking for me. Christ! I've lost his tea can." Tea was the engineman's life blood when he couldn't get ale. Joe shuddered at the magnitude of his error. How'd he explain his carelessness. "I've left his billycan near that Cudworth wagon. I'd better go and get it before it gets blown up."

"Daft sod. Yuh can't go there now. It'll be a bloody inferno now."

"I'm goin'. Got to go and let me mate know."

"Yuh can't."

"Wanna bet. I'll run down this empty road. I'll be alright. Jingo's at the other end of Singleton's locked in with the derailment. There's two full roads between this one and the fire."

"Stop aboard son. I'll take you down there on the engine. I might as well be as far away as possible. There's a phonebox down there"

Joe ran off to throw the points over so that the engine could run down the empty road and soon he and the crew were travelling as fast as the saddletank's little wheels would carry them. They couldn't get out of the other end of the empty road because the derailed wagon was standing foul.

"Where's me tea?" Jingo's first words greeted Joe as he boarded the D20.

"Up there. I'll get it soon." he wiped a black hand over the smarting eye and lip. 'What the hell do I do to always be in bloody difficulty', he thought.

"That wagon on our train is burning like hell."

"I can see sommat's burning. Like bloody Krakatoa."

"Jingo, the wagons, those in the next road to ours, are full of explosives an',,, they're alongside the burning wagon," he gabbled excitedly. "They're for Church Fenton airfield."

"What're they doing about it?" Jingo's response was calm. 'No alarm,' noted Joe, 'hope he's like this when he learns that his tea can's blown up.'

"They want us to push the train back up the feeder road and leave the burning wagon clear of the explosives," spluttered Joe, making it up as he thought quickly.

"Okay. Unpin the brakes on them first two wagons and I'll push back twenty wagon lengths. Is everyone clear at the far end?"

"Yes. Give a good whistle when yer move. I'll go and tell the saddle tank driver what we're doing." He hoped Jingo wouldn't mistake his purposeful instruction for insubordination. But, 'After all is said and done,' he thought, 'I've got to try and save his bloody tea can, else the rest of the day'll be hell.'

The saddle tank driver agreed and went to telephone Milford signal box and the shunter's cabin.

Jingo had to sand his rails and exert his engine. The driving wheels slipped and spun until the load grudgingly moved in spite of the blazing Cudworth wagon being firmly braked. The lack of exploding ammunition wagons seemed to prove that their efforts had been successful.

When the wagon was pushed well clear Joe announced that he'd go and fetch the billycan.

"Yes and go across to Milford Cabin," Jingo interjected. "Ask what plans Control has for us? I'd told the slops I'd see 'em at tea-time at home."

'Slops' was current vernacular for police in Castlebrough. Joe knew that but would like to have known more about why Jingo should be seeing the police. He nodded and ran off to see the state of play with the burning wagon and, with a prayer on his lips, look for Jingo's billycan.

A Green Goddess fire engine had managed to drive down the rough grassed perimeter of the yard to gain proximity to the burning wagon. The firefighters had extinguished the blaze without any of the oil or kerosene barrels exploding. That had been crucial. The wagon was destroyed but the permanentway was little harmed. The marshalling yard would not be closed as it would have been if more extensive damage had occurred.

"Good thing your mate done. Pushin' clear like that. There'd a been a big bang if he hadna." Just one of the comments that fell on Joe's ears as he mixed with the crowd of railwaymen who hung curiously around the burnt-out wagon. There was general approval of the Castlebrough man's quick action.

Joe was relieved. He'd found his mate's can unharmed near the scorched ammo boxvans and he'd added boiling water to the undisturbed tea leaves. He'd succeeded without losing Jingo's can but it had been a close call. Milford Signal cabin assured Joe that they would soon be off. "Leave your D20 where it's blocked in and pick up Q6 3395 from Selby men on the down side of the yard where it's on pilot duty. They'll be picking up your D20 when it's free". Joe guessed that would please Jingo who wanted to get home for either a medical or to see the 'slops'. 'Had he really meant the police?' Joe queried inwardly.

* * * * * *

2
JIMMY IN THE SMOKE-BOX

The four Castlebrough men were on Jim Simpson's J27 tender engine by the turntable and water column on the south side of the mainline that cut the marshalling yard in two. Jimmy Simpson, Castlebrough Town's sole Labour Councillor, to give him his social status and correct name, was articulating on the course of the War.

"Should be over by Christmas if the Second Front's launched this spring."

"What do you know about war? Yuh missed the last lot. Still a babby in nappies tha' was while I was at the Somme, keeping foreigners out. One thing Kitchener found out, make your plans and don't promise an end result."

"Jim's right," interjected Joe, "get our land forces into France, just o'er Channel an' Hitler 'll 'ave to throw the towel in."

"You should've thrown the towel in last night," grinned Jingo Johnson teasingly touching Joe's swollen left side with a straight left flick. He was forever riding Joe about his politics and what a waste of time it all was. This time he changed the subject.

Simpson's fireman Johnny Marsay, tried to feed the political debate, he, like Joe, was stimulated by the great upheaval that was changing the world. He liked a deep debate on literature, politics, and, like all railwaymen, about railways. But Jingo wasn't having any serious political discussion, he knew he was outnumbered politically by the three.

"Guy Reynolds didn't do that to you did he now? More like yuh tried it on with some tart," jibed Jingo.

"Truth is yes, and truth is no. I did five sparring rounds with my mate Jim Peckett yesterday afternoon in his front room, he's taken out a professional licence and he's fighting at York Racecourse on Saturday."

"You're mate did that?" enquired Simpson.

"No Jim. He just patted me about a bit and dodged my right crosses and straight lefts. His current training programme is developing a defence against a straight left and right cross."

"If he didn't who did? More like some tart's handbag as I said," grinned Jingo's long dour face.

"I went to club after tea, just to socialise. Not to get in the ring. Mike Carsay wouldn't leave me alone. 'Come on Joe,' he sez. 'Yuh owes me a round.' I had a tap about with him. Then Guy

Reynolds, who'd been on the punch ball, jumped in the ring and dared me to give him a spin. 'Won't hurt yuh son. Just move fast and throw all yuh've got at me.' He didn't hurt me, just leathered me face and left me thinkin' it were firework night. Didn't hurt me, though."

"This is getting boring. Thought yuh were boxing, it sounds more like you were both knitting." Joe ignored his driver's jibes.

"Then Mike Carsey got in the ring. 'Next round to me Joe,' he said. I wouldn't say no even though I was buggered. We'd just started and he was backin' away when I tapped his nose. He fell back towards the ropes and catapulted off them. His glove exploded in my face and I was going through the ropes at the other side on me back and clouted the floor with me face. Knocked myself out I did."

"The floor sort off came up and hit yer eye and mouth," laughed Johnny.

"Sort of Johnny."

"Some tail our cat's got. Yuh could've said yuh ran into a door." said Jingo.

"Your engine's coming." interrupted Jim. "He's backing over the pit on top of us. That'll put you in front Jingo, for going back. Is that alright?"

"Alright by me, Jim. We'll get back quicker wi' me clouting on at the front. There's about 70 on going back, most of them sixteen tonners. I want to get back soon so I can pacify His Majesty's Police."

"What's that to do with?" asked Jim Simpson. "Is it to do about the robbery last Thursday?"

"I'm sort of the main suspect." Jingo answered without emotion.

Johnny Marsay changed the subject."Looks like a right old load a crap they've brought for you to be clouting back with," he said looking from the cab at the ancient, dusty Q6 tender locomotive that was backing up to them. "They 've dredged it up from the ark."

The four of them left Simpson's J27 and examined the Q6 loco after the Selby men had departed. It was designed for hauling heavy loads at moderate speed. 'It should be better than the D20 for hauling 70 loaded coal wagons back to Castlebrough,' thought Joe. But there the optimism ended. The cab was filthy, still sooty from when the engine had been lit from cold, and dust-covered from fire ash, one water gauge glass was shut off because a bottom washer had blown. The clack was blowing on the right hand injector, wasting valuable steam, the fire was blue with clinker, and that was far from the end of the catalogue of misery.

"See if we've any oil and detonators and flags. Check the headlamps for kerosene. We ain't goin' to get back before dark. Put the tarpaulin up, then it's up, bloody mess, this lot." Jingo grumbled on.

Joe felt decidedly depressed. He was feeling the cold. His head was far from clear, his eye was puffing up more and his swollen lip and cheek had made drinking and chewing difficult and painful. A look in the fire-box told him he'd better clean the fire before setting off on the long journey back to Castlebrough. That wouldn't normally have presented much difficulty but the badly misshapen, curled up state of the clinker shovel, and of other fire-irons made it a difficult task. With the use of Johnny Marsay's fire-irons he effected some sort of improvement to the fire, but he had neither the will nor the energy to make a good job.

One-thirty in the afternoon and the two engines were coupled to 71 coal wagons waiting for the exit board to give them permission to start, hopefully, on their journey home with the desperately needed coal for Castlebrough's gas and electricity works. The hard winter had caused coal stocks to become depleted. That was reason why Jingo and Joe had been instructed to double-head the morning coal train. The gasworks were operating well below normal capacity and pressure to domestic users had been drastically reduced.

"She's not steaming very well George," Joe shouted to Jingo who had the steam regulator wide open. They were only eight miles into their journey and approaching Copmanthorpe on the road to York. The boiler was half-empty and the engine was priming. The boiler water was so cloudy and effervescent in the water-gauge glass that Joe was unsure of the true level, all he knew was that he hadn't put any water into the boiler since they had started from Gascoigne Wood.

Jingo didn't respond. He had a Players filter-tip cigarette in his mouth, his liking for better class cigarettes marked him off a little from the general run of loco men at the shed. Mostly they smoked Woodbine or Park Drive cigarettes or rolled their own, or smoked assorted twists in pipes. Jingo would smoke nothing but Players.

Jingo seemed not to be interested in Joe's plight. Joe knew of his attitude to his relationship with a fireman, "You mek the steam and I use it," he was fond of saying. On the present occasion Jingo just kept his eye on the road and appeared deep in thought. His only conversation with Joe since leaving Gascoigne Wood had been to comment on the engine's tendency to prime.

Joe knew that this meant that water was flowing from the boiler down the steam pipes into the cylinders and if it did no harm it was expelled up through the blast-pipe and out through the chimney. If it did its worst, as it could do, it would burst a cylinder-end out and the engine would have to be failed.

They were on the slow line into York, and quite obviously tailing a slow moving goods train. Expresses flashed past on the mainline as the coal train continued its slow progress in the same direction. The constant steam shut-offs helped Joe to maintain steam but the water level fell dramatically. When they approached York, boiler pressure was down to 100lb, hardly enough to keep going.

Some drivers would have taken to trying to do something to help the fireman but not Jingo. He did what he was paid for, he'd served his time on the end of the shovel, now he was the driver. He didn't have to tell this to Joe, the shed grapevine, on which fireman and cleaners discoursed about their drivers, told Joe what to expect from Jingo.

"You're farting about with that shovel aren't you?"

"I ain't. It's the engine. It's no good. Fire's mucky. There isn't much blast on the fire. An' like you said it's priming badly."

"Bloody excuses. How we goin' to make Castlebrough, forty-five miles away when you're flat out after fifteen miles." He paused. Joe had no idea what to reply. "An' it don't get no better," added Jingo.

"Bollocks," Joe said loud enough for his mate to hear but either Jingo didn't or he chose to ignore the meaningless outcry. As if to add further pain to Joe's injury Jim Simpson's J27 loco started to blow off unwanted steam.

"We're being put inside the reception sidings." Jingo gave a pop on his whistle as he passed the distant signal at caution position. Jim Simpson popped back in acknowledgement. They drew to a slow halt in one of the long sidings not far from the renowned large 'Locomotive Yard ' signal cabin of 234 levers controlling the southern approaches to York. A little further on they could see the huge arched York station roof.

"What do yuh say is wrong, son?"

"Dunno really except that the fire's dirty. Watter's mucky in the boiler, that's mekin' her prime, as you said. There's no blast on the fire. Even the blower's weak."

"Yuh ain't got a camel's hump in the middle 'ave yuh?"

"No."

"Is yuh damper working?"

"Dunno really, never looked. Seems to work when I pull on the handle."

"Did yer check your smoke-box door?"

"No, Should I have done?"

"Don't they teach you anything at those mutual improvement classes."

"Course they do." Joe felt and looked a little sheepishly.

"Let's have a look at things." Jingo was brusque. "They're letting young kids go on engines before they know how to find their own arses."

Joe didn't reply, just got out of the way. He followed Jingo's instructions. He pulled up and down on the damper handle while Jingo looked between the wheel spokes through the damper door and into the ash pan.

Jingo then looked into the fire-box. "A bit of brick-arch down. Tubeplate all scarred up. Some of it's clinkered up. Have a look."

Joe squatted down on the footplate in front of the open fire-door. "Yuh see the scar on the tubeplate. Yuh see that some tubes is blocked?" continued Jingo. "Look at the lead fusible plugs. Yuh know where they are don't yuh? See if they're leaking or blowing." Joe looked up at the roof of the fire-box. Of course he knew where the lead plugs were. They weren't leaking Thank God. He didn't want blaming for dropping his lead plugs and flooding the firebox.

"Come on now, open the smoke-box, but put your jet blower on first. Put it on hard." Joe was doing things because Jingo was telling him, not because he knew what he was doing. "Bring your coal hammer and firing shovel."

Outside on the footplate at the front end of the loco Jingo felt around the periphery of the tightly shut circular smoke-box door. He was feeling for draught being pulled in by the drag of the jet stream blowing in the smoke-box. "Engine won't steam proper if the smoke-box door is letting air in," Jingo explained. "Go and turn your jet off now," he ordered Joe. "Then come back and open the smoke-box." Joe obliged and when the large circular door was open Jingo continued. "See the blast-pipe," he said, "no carbon in it. It's had a de-coke or a new blast-pipe fitted. That's why there's no blast on the fire when we running. Get a bucket of dry sand from the rear sandboxes, back boxes mind you, not front boxes.

Might need the the front sands. Shut yer smoke-box and come back into the cab."

Joe was fed up. He felt that he was wasting time when he should have been trying to raise steam for the journey that faced them. Back in the engine cab he noticed Jingo running off some of the water from the tap on the engine tender into his white billycan. After an examination of the water in his can he instructed Joe. "Start cleaning your fire, I'm going up to Loco Box. I want to find a 'Jimmy' and find out how long we've got here."

Joe was too fed up to ask any questions. He borrowed the long clinker shovel and fire-irons from Johnny, from whom he gained a promise of help. He appreciated the offer because he didn't feel in a fit state to be struggling to remove clinker from a hot fire or extracting dry sand from the long necked sandboxes.

"We're going to be stuck here 'til three-thirty," Jingo said by way of announcing his presence in the cab where Joe and Johnny were working when he arrived. "We'll put a 'Jimmy' in the smoke-box before you make the fire up and fill the smoke-box with smoke." Joe didn't ask any questions. He didn't want to show his ignorance although, without asking, he guessed that a 'Jimmy' in the smoke-box had nothing to do with Jimmy Simpson on the other engine.

Without doing much of the work Jingo supervised a series of operations designed to make his engine function more efficiently. The one that held Joe's greatest interest was fitting the 'Jimmy' in the smoke-box. Jingo did this as if it was some secret rite, he gave no explanation. Joe did not seek one, he carried out Jingo Johnson's instructions without question.

Jingo had acquired about three-feet of soft copper quarter-inch oil lubrication pipe from some undescribed source nearby. On instruction Joe opened the large circular smoke-box at the forward end of the engine boiler. The three-foot vertical blast-pipe with about a six - inch bore, in the centre of the circular chamber, was the object of Jingo's intentions. He twisted the length of copper tube around the top edge of the blast-pipe just below the jet ring, and then crossed over the diameter of the blast-pipe; much like a child would wrap wool around a cotton bobbin and then cross over the diameter of the hole in preparation for french knitting. "That'll do," was his only comment about the 'Jimmy' he had fitted. "Fasten the smoke-box door as tight as you can get it. Don't want it letting air in?"

Joe was next directed to clear his ash pan and make the damper door so it would open as far as possible. Then Jingo did one job he wouldn't trust to Joe. He took Johnny's long clinker shovel, placed it in the fire-box, but not on the fire bars. Instead he riskily rested the blade on the brick arch which spanned the width of the fire-box to protect the tube plate. Then he manipulated the long metal shovel to remove the clinker scar which clung to the tube plate and blocked off some of the tubes. "Don't do that ever. It's bloody tricky. You can bring the brick arch down if you're unlucky," he told Joe as he withdrew the shovel. "Start making you're fire up and raise steam. We're going to drain the tender water off and refill at yon water crane." He opened an injector feed valve on the tender and the water commenced draining way. "I think York water will be cleaner than the Selby river water we've got."

The tricks weren't over yet Joe learnt as Jingo showed him the use he intended for the bucket of dry sand. With the blower at full blast Jingo tossed small shovelfuls of dry sand high into the fire-box towards the tube plate. The cloud of sand scoured through the tubes and propelled a black cloud of particles out of the chimney high into the sky.

"Like blowing sand through the chimney at home to clean it." said Jingo and then continued until most of the sand had gone. "Do it again a few times when we are on the road."

"Is that all?" returned Joe.

"I'll show you another one but it's quite dangerous. Don't you try until you've had a lot more experience." He picked up the fireman's shovel and held the blade out towards Joe. "Pour about half a pint of paraffin on there and put the blower on as hard as she'll go. Stand well back in case we get a blow-back." He balanced the paraffin on the shovel and, suddenly and deftly, delivered it quickly into the fire-box. The paraffin vaporised in the fire-box and exploded causing a flashback tongue of flame into the cab. They looked through the window and saw an even denser black cloud floating skyward. Then he did it again and again. "Should steam a little better now."

"Thanks George."

George grinned. "It ain't all to be found in books. Jimmies for instance are illegal, not allowed I mean."

"What will it do?"

"Yuh know how the exhaust steam blasts up through the blast-pipe and chimney and causes a draught on the fire. A jimmy splits the blast and makes it more powerful. A bit like putting a smaller nozzle on a garden hose."

"Why are they not allowed, illegal?"

"Main reason is that some men make their own that can be screwed on and taken off. Sometimes they get dropped down the blast-pipe and jam in the valves and the steam chest."

"I'm blinking hungry George." said Joe with a nod of appreciation for the knowledge Jingo had just imparted.

"So am I. We'll fill the tank then you can walk into the station and get me a meat pie from the men's canteen."

"When will we get a road, George?"

"He said about three-thirty. I'll check when we get watter."

Joe and his mate went to the Locomotive Yard signal cabin where four signalmen operated the 234 manual vertical levers in the long frame. Joe had been in this box before but each time it fascinated him, it was so large. The cabin looked out onto what seemed acres of lines and a forest of semaphore signals.

Three-thirty it was to be. "Traffic was slackening," the chargeman signalman said. "If nowt untoward happens I should be able to give you a road after the Castlebrough express leaves No 9 at three-twenty-five. When you're over the Ouse you should be lucky and make a run to Malton before you're stopped. You'll be on overtime now aren't you?" the signalman asked Jingo.

"Don't know about overtime. I'll be doing time after this little lot today," Jingo responded.

"What's happened today?"

"Bloody late that's what."

"Yeh but Castlebrough Coalie always runs late. What's that to do with doin' time?" Joe's ears sharpened at the reference to 'doing time'. It fitted in with the earlier comment on 'Slops' and the snatches of conversations he'd overheard in the messroom that morning about the bond cage being broken into at Castlebrough Goods station.

"I've been helping the slops with their inquiries," grinned Jingo's long face."I told them I'd see them again at about four today."

"Why time?"

"I think I'm the main suspect," Jingo grinned back at the interested signalman.

"Main suspect? In a cigs and drinks robbery?" echoed Joe.

"You still 'ere. Thought I'd told you to go and fetch two meat pies from the station canteen. Go on now, get some steam coming out of your arse. You've only got twenty minutes, and don't get flamin' lost."

Joe had to move fast and subdue his burning desire to discover further missing pieces in the slowly assembling jigsaw of Jingo's brush with the police. Without trouble he made his way down the complex permanent way towards York station, having to take care to avoid the moving locos and trains that made their passages through the lines and signals.

Number eight platform teemed with passengers and railway staff. He threaded his way through the crowd occupied only by his thoughts which were suddenly ruptured by what he saw. Joe moved forwards more urgently, his heart began pounding, almost missing beats he thought. The object of his excitement was the station tea trolley, surrounded by servicemen and passengers who were about to board the passenger train to London on platform eight.

'It can't be? She'd be at school, wouldn't she? Or could she have left school and got a job?' The questions poured through his mind. Then statements and affirmations followed. 'Yes, it's like her. It is Carol. She's serving tea to passengers. She's got a railway uniform on. Yes, I'd know that red hair anywhere, that nose, even those eyes.'

"Watch out mate. That's my case you're kicking."

Joe stumbled, muttered his sincerest apologies and went to join the band of prospective customers at the trolley. It was like a fight. The pushing and shoving, and the "I'm before you pal" managed to halt Joe's approach to the trolley. But he was convinced it was Carol, he heard her distant voice announce loudly, "All the pies have gone. Don't wait just for a pie."

"Bloody pies." Joe spoke out aloud.

"What's that Mister?"

"All the pies have gone, son." he informed the schoolboy at his elbow. But he knew he hadn't just been repeating Carol's announcement, he'd been expressing alarm at the realisation that his errand was to buy two pies from the staff canteen. He elbowed his way out and made off towards the canteen as quickly as the obstacles would allow.

"Dam it. A bloody queue." Joe looked around for a wall clock in the canteen room and saw the time to be three-twenty-five. 'Hell, they'll be pulling off for Jingo soon,' he agitated inwardly. 'Can't stand in a queue of twenty people.' He walked straight to the front, alarmed by, but ignoring, the manifestations of impatience by the others in the queue. He raised the waitress' access point in the counter and made to go through.

"You can't come in here son. You're too dirty for one thing."

"But. - - but."

"But what ? You can't come in." repeated the motherly figure behind the counter.

"I was looking for my Aunty Bet," Joe blurted.

"Bet who?"

"Bet Wade."

"No Bet Wade. There's Bet Smith, but she's not on now."

"Of course, I forgot her married name. Can't get used to the idea that she's married."

"She's still not here son."

"I was only going to ask her to get me two pies. You see I'm the fireman on that London train in eight platform and we pull out in two minutes. Me and my mate haven't eaten for eight hours an' I can't afford to stand in that queue."

"Why didn't you say? Here's two pies. Be off. No, don't pay. Bet'll see to that. You her nephew? Who shall I say?"

"Joe. Just say Joe, Fred's lad. And thanks. You've just saved the London express." He produced a painful grin. He ran out onto the platform. 'Wish I really had an Aunt Bet, she's a good sort,' thought Joe amazed at his own sheer cheek.

He couldn't ignore Carol. She was more accessible now. He pushed up towards her tea trolley, caught her eye momentarily, and winked his damaged eye. The pain made him grimace. She looked curiously at his black swollen face. He self-consciously cast his eyes down, then winked his good eye. "You know me." he tried to say to her amid the clamour of orders.

"I've only scones left," she said to all who were listening but gave another sideways queer look to Joe, who unfortunately suffered a jostle from behind and had is cap pushed forward over his eyes. A blast on the London train engine whistle brought him back to the railway reality.

'God that's the three-thirty to London,' he thought, 'Jingo'll be getting his signal.' He scrambled through the figures on the platform as quickly as possible in the direction of the reception sidings. The London train pulled out of platform eight in a mighty clamour of belching smoke and steam. It left Joe with a clear view of the lines in front of Locomotive Box. A goods train was pulling out towards York station's through mainline, its headlights glimmered, showing that they had been lighted and that there was a hint of dusk about. The position of the headlights indicated that the train was a class 'F' goods, two columns of smoke and steam spouting slowly skywards at the fore-end of the train betrayed that it was double-headed.

"Bloody hell! Without me? Never thought he'd go without me?" He was talking to himself out loud and nearby passengers registered the fact by turning their heads. The two pies, wrapped loosely in one piece of paper, were dropped unceremoniously into his overall jacket pockets, one in each pocket, one without paper. He ran off in the direction of his departing train, grateful that it was coming in his direction, thus the gap between him and his loco was decreasing.

Running along the icy permanentway; with signal wires, point rods, ground dollies, junction boxes, signal gantries, and amid moving rail stock was a risky business at the best of times. Running on ice and snow with your mate's treasured meat pie in your pocket and then leaping aboard his passing locomotive was all the more hazardous to say the least. Joe dare not think it, what if he should crush his mate's pie, and, he reminded himself, his mate was the rough Jingo. He positioned himself alongside the track that carried the oncoming Castlebrough coal train. He tried not to be distracted by a fast goods train that was now coming at a fair speed from the through main just eight feet away from him.

Jingo had seen him. The steam was shut off from both engines, they coasted whilst Joe grabbed the passing cold handrail to be plucked by the engine's speed from the ice-covered track. His feet found the passing step and his arms pulled him aboard. Jingo had seen Joe hauling himself aboard but now he had his head out of his own cab window; he was searching for all the signals that applied to his road through York station. Joe hastily extracted the two unprotected pies from his pocket and wrapped the smallest one in the piece of crumpled paper and handed it over. He justified his decision to give Jingo the slightly smaller pie with the thought that 'I'm a growing lad. An' I do all the work.'

"Bloody idiot, where did yuh get to? You've been a bloody week."

"Queuing George. Bloody big queue. I was too hungry to give up. An' I knew you were hungry." He cut the conversation short by picking up his firing shovel and having a look into his fire-box. As they passed through the station and under the bridge near the canteen and the booking hall he looked towards Carol and her trolley. Joe waved. She did not notice. She was in conversation with the motherly lady in the canteen who knew Aunty Betty. Joe shouted. The motherly lady looked and, with a vague indication that she knew him, waved back, probably thinking, 'He looks a bit like that fireman that went out on the London Train with two pies.'

Carol still hadn't looked with any acknowledgement so Joe grabbed the whistle cord and gave a loud blast on the engine whistle.

"What the bloody hell are yer doing?" Jingo burst out.

"Platelayer on the track down here, was givin' him a warning we was coming," lied Joe. He loved blowing engine whistles. He was always transgressing the unwritten code, 'that the driver blows the whistle except in emergency.' Joe had a well developed sense of what comprises an emergency so he could pop the whistle whenever he wanted.

Carol looked and he waved, but she waved back just like any member of the public. The double-headed coal train, filling the station roof with, smoke, steam and noise, attracted a lot of attention and many of the figures on the platform waved and showed interest. Joe was not satisfied that she had seen him.

Jingo called out to Joe. "See this loco on nine. Do you recognise it?"

"Mallard!" The word shot out as his eyes fell on the well-known World-famous streamlined A4 Pacific locomotive that held the World steam train speed record. "I know of her. 126 miles per hour she did in 1938. I'd like to fire her" he said with admiration. "What's she doing there on nine platform?"

"Earning her living. She's working London to Edinburgh."

"One day I'll get on her when she's passing through York."

"Yeh, but for now you're on here," Jingo added sarcastically. "Stick yer bloody head out o' that side, see if all the dollies are off for over Castlebrough Bridge. Then look at yer fire." He paid attention to the signals on the gantries then turned again to Joe. "We want to get through to Malton before we get stopped for an express. So keep the steam pressure up. Don't fart about like a schoolboy, get stuck in"

* * * * * *

3
WHERE THERE'S SMOKE THERE'S FIRE

The shadows were already beginning to lengthen, giving an indication that blackout-time was not far away and that the rest of their journey to Castlebrough would be in the dark. Joe knew that the line to Malton was twenty-one miles into the darkness and that the first ten miles were slightly rising gradients that would cause him to work hard. There would be no let up, no rallies for steam, Jingo would keep hammering away at the Q6 locomotive with a full open regulator; he'd want to get home for a pint in the Railway Tavern. Joe knew the pattern.

He checked all the ground signals along their path onto the long iron 'Castlebrough Bridge' that spanned the wide River Ouse. "Okay George," he shouted and gave a thumbs-up sign to his mate at the other side of the cab. He knew Jingo would know from his mainline semaphore signals that the road would be set and clear, and that he couldn't see around the curve of the track; he knew that Jingo was just using him to keep a second pair of eyes on the track.

They had the road. Jim Simpson and Jingo behaved accordingly. Their two engine chimneys shot their noisy blasts skywards, they knew that the long coal train was slowly snaking behind them and blocking both the up and down mainlines through York. They'd clear the tracks they were blocking as soon as was humanly possible, that was their unwritten code.

Joe felt the old surge of pride and achievement. He wasn't on an express, he was merely firing a very old badly maintained L.N.E.R. locomotive that wouldn't steam, but he was essential. The lights and energy of Castlebrough depended upon him getting his train through; he was just as important to the war effort as any soldier, maybe more so.

The two locos crossed the long iron and stone bridge which seemed to groan and sag under their combined weight. The eternal song of wheel against rail sang on a different scale. The boards were off down the high brick-walled cutting that started the road to Castlebrough, little green signal lights were just beginning to twinkle and indicate that daylight was receding. Joe put his head out of his cab window into the cold air and listened to the music of the thumping and exerting engines accompanied by Jingo's long blast on his engine whistle and Jimmy's answering shorter blast.

"Put the rest of the sand through the tubes now," Jingo yelled across the cab breaking into Joe's reverie.

Joe looked into his fire-box, noted that the fire was brighter than before and tossed little clouds of sand high into the fire-box to scour the tubes on their passage to the smoke-box and the atmosphere. He nervously started to deliver coal to his firebed; well to the front, down each side, then into the back end. He fired according to textbook instructions. He noted that Jingo had the regulator wide open in full second port, he knew also that he'd need all his skill to keep Jingo supplied with steam.

The miles slowly thundered by, the sky darkened and stars became visible between patches of cloud, the engines' whistles kept piercing the night as the two driver's responded to whistle boards, or distant signals displaying caution, or signalmen waving from their cabins. Passing trains screamed in the direction of York with a sudden roar on the neighbouring line.

The engine steamed better as a result of Jingo's doctoring, the 'Jimmy' cut the exhaust blast in the smoke-box causing a more powerful blast of air to be pulled through the fire and consume coal faster. Despite all Joe's efforts the water level fell in the single working gauge glass, he had to sacrifice his water to maintain steam at 175 pounds pressure. The occasional rally as Jingo was forced to shut off steam when caution signals or a red light faced them in the distance gave Joe slight respite but he had to keep his shovel busy in spite of his tired back and aching head. He looked down the train as it rounded the bend approaching Kirkham Abbey, he was looking back at the sheeted second engine to see if his mate Johnny had his head out. Johnny was there, his capped head gently illuminated by his cab's firelight glow, his engine blew off steam from it's safety valves as if mocking Joe and his shortage.

"He's got steam to spare George. He's blowing off" Joe reached forward and tapped Jingo on the shoulder that obtruded from the cab just in front of Joe. "Wish we could borrow some," he shouted.

Jingo's head turned. "We can. Put your jet on." He drew himself into cab. As Joe turned on his engine's jet blower Jingo closed his steam regulator. "We'll let him work on his own for a bit seeing he's so flush." He gave a blast on the engine whistle as they passed Kirkham Abbey's distant signal in clear position.

"Son," Jingo addressed Joe again. "Did you see we've got two hot boxes."

Joe went to Jingo's side again and looked back down the length of his train. He didn't need Jingo to point them out, he could see the two burning axle-boxes twinkling away part way back down the length of their train. "We'll have to stop and put them off. Wont we?" Joe questioned Jingo.

"Yeh. But with luck they'll let us run through to Malton. We'll know when we see Castle Howard's distant signal."

Jingo provided Joe with a well earned respite and Joe thought 'I didn't ask for it so it doesn't count as a rally.' Nevertheless the opportunity helped Joe increase his boiler water level by operating both his water injectors together before Jingo opened up again They ran through Castle Howard and Hutton's Ambo stations without a stop and Joe's engine coasted into the Malton goods reception line with little water and just over 100 pounds steam pressure.

"Loose off kidda. We'll run up into the coal yard and let Simpson shunt the two hot boxes out. It'll give you time to blow-up and fill up." They stood near the coal cells while Joe raked his fire with an assortment of irons, and then spent time sorting through the coal for lumps that might burn more easily. When Jim Simpson and his guard had shunted the two burning wagons and another one that was very hot and unlikely to complete the journey to Castlebrough, the two engines coupled to their train. The crews and the guard assembled on the footplate of Jingo's Q6 goods engine.

"You've missed the railway policeman George," said Jim Simpson.

"I've missed more than that. I was expecting to play for the Tavern Darts Team down at the Mere Social Club tonight."

"We've only taken an hour-and-twenty with this load from York," said Joe indicating the time with his Grandfather's watch.

"We'll be here for a good hour now waiting for the workmen's train and that Special to pass," grumbled the train guard. "Then if we hang about after we get away the eight-thirty York might catch up with us and that'll hold us back 'til ten o' clock."

"She's not steaming too well, is she Joe? Saw you coasting round those bends leaving us to do the work." Johnny's grinning interjection broke into Matt's groan about the lateness of their homeward journey.

"Not doing bad for an old one. We're managing. You were blowing off so we thought we'd let you use your waste steam," laughed Joe.

"What do the police want you for?" Johnny changed the subject as he addressed Jingo.

"They don't want me for anything. Just questions to help them trace six cartons o' fags that walked from the bond cage at Gallows Close last Thursday night when I was on night firewatch."

"Why you? There were others on firewatch," Johnny wondered out loud.

"I was on the same night George," chipped in Joe. "I came on late at ten o' clock. Saw you playing cards with Bill Ankler and a couple of porters. You stopped up and I went straight to bed."

"Six cartons of fags had been checked in to the bond cage and entered on the checking in sheet. They weren't there next morning."

"Was the cage broke into?" asked Johnny.

"No. That's what makes them think it was an inside job?" added Jingo.

"If the cage weren't broke into, how do they know they've been pinched."

"The checker's inward sheet recorded that they were taken out of a Newcastle van from Wills and checked into the bond cage. They were for the 'Tobacco Cabin' on North Street. They wonder if I knew anything about it because I walked round the warehouse late on Thursday night after the card game."

"Not much to go on George," said Jim Simpson.

"They don't need much to question you. They say where there's smoke there's fire. And they say I'm smoking," Jingo added, then to Joe. "Tek me tea can and see if the signalman's got a kettle on the boil."

Joe made off towards Malton West cabin, walking down the length of his train on the side away from the mainline. He'd seen the up line signals falling into clear position indicating that a train was due to approach Malton station. The night was pleasant in spite of the biting cold, the sounds of the river Derwent flowing southwards drifted across the field towards Joe, the faint moon hung slightly above the outline of the low hills to the east, the tall coal wagons accompanied him on his left. He enjoyed the walk through the crisp night and felt ease and rest flow into his tiring body. Thirteen hours had passed since he had signed on at five-fifteen that morning with Simpson, Johnny and Jingo for their special run to Gascoigne Wood. They still had a long haul to Castlebrough.

"Can I beg a brew from yuh, mister?" Joe asked as he walked into the cosy oil-lit signal cabin.

"Yes, she's just simmering. Top up and get back to your engine. The workmen's is coming through in a minute then we're going to let you go."

"Didn't expect that. My mate said you had a special coming through before we could go."

"It's lost a lot of time. Still at York. If you get cracking you might get to Castlebrough before him and before the eight-thirty York."

Joe raced back with the half-full billycan of slopping tea. The three loco men and the guard received the news joyfully. Joe livened his fire rapidly and added fresh coal. He knew that Jingo would have the scent of Moor and Robson's ale in his taste buds if not in his nostrils, and there would be no mercy for his fireman. The workmen's train duly passed and halted at Malton station leaving the line clear for the long coal train and two engines. The boiler was brimming and the Q6 loco's safety valves were shooting two columns of steam skywards as the exit signal dropped off and gave them passage from the siding onto the mainline. Two whistles blasted, in greeting and all signals through Malton changed to green.

They were off. Joe kept an ear alert for the sound that his engine might prime. He'd filled his boiler as high as he dared; it was a gamble that paid off. Jingo's wide open regulator valve failed to pick up the water and blast it through the cylinders and up the chimney. The pounding roar of the two heaving engines, the blast in the fire-box and the simmering safety valves were music in Joe's ears. He laboured away constantly, leaving the outside darkness to Jingo's eyes. He fired with his fire-hole door closed; each time his laden shovel swept towards the fire it struck the hanging blast deflector plate and kicked it open, allowing his coal load into the fire-box, and then fall shut. He'd learnt many tricks of the fireman's trade since his first mainline run with Bob Laker.

They roared happily through the night, more like an express train than a 'F' goods. Jingo had his engine on a low 35% steam cut off, making Joe work fast and furiously but the resulting roaring blast at the chimney top caused the fire to burn with a healthy white heat. Jim Simpson's J27 was likewise exerting every steel sinew and muscle and tossing hot coals from the chimney into the night sky.

Joe felt no anxiety as the boiler water level fell inexorably as he maintained his boiler pressure at close to blowing-off point, he just schemed to get the best out of his engine. He climbed over the coal boards into the rocking tender with his coal pick and excavated for lumps of better quality coal, keeping in mind all the time what a dangerous practice it was to be upright in the tender of a moving loco. He could get his brains knocked out, he knew, if his head level appeared above the cab roof. Occasional use of his long fire-irons on the tender top behind his anti-glare sheet caused him similar risks.

Jingo's eyes were out in the night probing for the little red, amber and green signal lights, observing every signal cabin for hand signals by the signalman or signal woman, picking out every accommodation crossing signal light. How small the lights were compared with road traffic lights. At every curve in the line Jingo looked back along the length of his train from both sides of his loco for burning axle-boxes or signals from his guard. He kept a questioning eye on the chimney of Jim Simpson's engine and the strength of blast coming out, indicating the amount of work being undertaken by the J27. He was satisfied.

Joe knew from the language of the track when they had passed through the roofed station of Rillington, and over culvert bridges, road crossings and by station platforms. He was learning the road by instinct, by alert senses, he had a good idea where they were even though he had not looked out since Malton.

"We've just passed Knapton haven't we George?" shouted Joe into Jingo's ear that was turned into the cab.

"Yes. Heslerton's back board just coming up. It's off." Jingo yelled triumphantly. "We've got the road clear to Weaverthorpe. We'll soon be seeing if we are going to get stopped at Weaverthorpe or Ganton. Put the blower on and get some watter in the boiler. I'll give you a rest while the gradients are slightly in our favour."

Joe's heart warmed to Jingo, who for so long had been on his 'list of nasty characters'. The water level was bobbing about in the bottom of the single water-gauge glass, steam pressure had fallen to 150 pounds pressure. Jingo hadn't complained, hadn't offered any advice since his diagnosis and help at York. Joe fired while they coasted with the blower doing the job of the blast and he added water to his depleted boiler.

They got their road through Weaverthorpe and Ganton without hindrance. The regulator opened up again with a low cut-off causing the chimney top to roar. They tore on with an increasing sense of urgency as the miles laboured past. Joe kept his head in the fire-lit cab, schemed at his task, and left the darkness and the hazards of the outside to Jingo and Jim Simpson. They slowed through Seamer and the bends approaching Castlebrough with very little water in sight in their glass. Boiler pressure was now down to a weak 100 pounds pressure and just keeping them going.

"Put your water on mate when we're passing Caxton's, Simmy 'll keep the brakes working." Being addressed as mate by Jingo and not 'kid' or 'kiddo' or 'son' struck Joe as some kind of promotion, he appreciated it and felt his chest stand out. He was just about to complete a fifteen-and- half-hour day and arrive back in Castlebrough at 8.30pm, well in front of the special and the York express. He'd earned the accolade 'mate' from the normally unsympathetic and inexpressive Jingo. He felt great, even though he really felt quite ill and exhausted.

"Howdy," said Bill Clarke to Jingo, who was first off the pair of engines that pulled into number one road of Castlebrough loco shed.

"Yeh," grunted Jingo, not necessarily unpleasant but clearly impatient to be on his way without hindrance.

"Are you in a rush?"

"Daft question just an hour before closing. Why?"

"Franker's in the messroom. Said he'd like to see you before you go home."

"Sod it! I've just made my sheet out and signed off. I'm not talking to the gaffer in me own time. Tell him to leave it until tomorrow."

"You tell him George. He came in special to see you."

"I'll tell him," stormed George as he set of into the badly-lighted shed.

"Have you made my mate angry, Bill?" asked Joe as he approached and witnessed Jingo bustling away.

"No, there's the gaffer and the railway policeman in the messroom to see Jingo. He's mad 'cause he wants to be off. Don't blame him. I'd be mad at the end of a fourteen hour shift."

"Fifteen and a half," corrected Joe.

Voices drifted through the heavy wooden door of the messroom as Joe, Jimmy, and Johnny approached and entered.

"Let's go up to my office, George?" Franker's voice suggested.

"No need to. I've had a bloody long day and I'm going." He leaned on the well-scrubbed white table with both hands and looked down at the seated and uncomfortable shed master and Maurice Wells the railway policeman for Castlebrough. He looked defiant and ready to be off whether they agreed or not.

"Sorry to have to catch you at the end of a long day, Mr Johnson but the office at York are crowding me for a report. They want me to bring the civil police in." The well-built Maurice had placed his trilby hat on the table, displaying an attitude that he was settling in for a long stay.

"I still think we should go to my office. It's too public here," injected Mr Franker.

"We'll get out of your way when we've signed off and checked the roster for tomorrow's work," broke in Jimmy Simpson who was conscious that his presence and that of Johnny Marsay and Joe were an embarrassment to the trio in discussion.

"No need to go for me. I'm off anyway." Jingo turned and moved towards the direction of the single doorway. He had second thoughts, and addressed himself to Jim. "They're accusing me of nicking six boxes of fags from Gallows Close last Thursday night when I was firewatching."

"I'm not." Mr Franker's firm statement somehow seemed to set him apart from the railway policeman."

"He is!"

"I'm not, either." Maurice Well's statement didn't sound quite so convincing.

"We'll go," said Jim Simpson, "Unless George wants us present. It's as well to have company or representations at times like this."

"I don't want company or representations unless - -" and he paused, "Unless they plan to stitch me up."

"Nothing like that George." Franker was emphatic and his voice expressed itself in a soft and sympathetic tone. "To speak honestly George you might just as well have Jim Simpson present. He's the N.U.R. chairman and one of your rep's on the shed L.D.C."

"Let 'em all stop. I'll stop five minutes to sort out what your problem is then I'm off." George was not the type to be cajoled, pressurised or subordinated, he was more likely to do these things to others.

Police Constable Wells took the opportunity to be forthright and get to the point. "You know I've got a job to do George. You've been questioned about the robbery last Thursday when you were firewatching. Unfortunately George you're our main suspect."

"Bloody hell! You amaze me. How on earth do you think I'm involved?"

"We needn't go too deeply into that just now except to say I've got to make a report to the York sergeant tomorrow and before I do I've got to check things with you."

"Check what with me?"

"What's in your possession? In your engine locker? In your messroom locker? You won't mind that will you?"

"You want to search me? Bloody frisk me? Like you're the Gestapo?"

"Look in that locker," he pointed to one of the two-foot square wooden wall lockers provided for engine men. "Number thirteen. That's yours isn't it?"

"Go to bloody hell! You and him too," he said indicating Franker with his cocked thumb.

"Bloody hell," gasped Joe. Jim Simpson placed a hand on the table and moved forward slightly as if he was about to express some concern.

"You all keep out o' this," Maurice Wells seemed to warn. "The locker's railway property, we can get a key and look in but we'd rather look in with your approval."

"You look but you're wont have my approval."

"Well let's look and get it over with."

"Do you think union's 'll approve? Jim."

"Don't think so George. I think Head Office would think all this a bit high handed. You're in A.S.L.E.F. I'm in N.U.R. You'll have to get on to them."

"I will. Too high handed for me. Bit like Hitler's mob."

"Come off it George. That's a bit heavy. P.C. Wells can open your locker without you being present. I asked him to wait while you were here. He's got authority to search anywhere on L.N.E.R. property without even my agreement."

Jingo demonstrated some impatience and moved around showing some agitation. "What yuh looking for?" he asked rather loudly with his eye falling on the plain clothes policeman.

"Cigs, pipe tobacco and a quantity of flake."

"Well, I've got a few cigs in there. I alus have a few cigs here if I've got any extra. I've got two lads at home who'll do anything for a smoke."

"Shall we have a look then?" P.C. Wells turned his eyes towards the door as a set of Castlebrough loco men entered. "Can we just have another minute before you come in?" he said in their direction.

"We wont be a minute Ernie" said Franker. "Can you go next door to Bill's place?"

Jingo was opening his number thirteen locker, his lanky body slightly crooked and his long face immobile, almost expressionless.

Joe felt a well of sympathy for Jingo, even a flush of gratitude for his help and guidance with the Q6. 'No man deserves this kind of humiliation' he thought and then wondered if slippery Jingo was going to pull one over his adversaries.

The pile of locoman's gear that appeared on the messroom table was what was to be expected. But the three packets of Player's cigarettes seemed to point a finger. It was not easy to acquire three packets of cigarettes unless they resulted from a special opportunity.

"So what? They're mine."

"Coupled with the cart and other evidence this means we are going to have to have a more serious discussion and involve the civilian police," Maurice Wells said softly in the direction of Mr Franker.

"What's 'the cart'?"

"Your brother Charles' decorator's handcart, it was at the goods yard on the night in question and was seen being pushed away from the yard in the early hours."

Joe intervened unexpectantly, "That was me. I took the cart to the goods yard."

"My ten minutes is up. Do what the hell you like, I'm going." Jingo's statement followed Joe's remark so quickly that what he said seemed to have gone almost unnoticed.

"Okay, you'd better go now but as I've arranged with Mr Franker you'll have to see us, me and the civilian police, tomorrow."

"You'll get the day off tomorrow, even though the roster shows you to be on back-turn coal pilot." added Mr Franker.

"We'd better see what this young fellow has to say as well. Did you say you took the cart to the goods yard?"

"Yes" said Joe addressing P.C. Wells. "I was on firewatching that night with Jingo. I mean George."

"Okay. You'd better come to the goods yard with Mr Johnson at two o'clock." He turned to the shed master, "Can you arrange that Mr Franker?" Franker nodded. Jingo had packed away his belongings in the locker minus the three packets which had found there way into the grasp of P.C. Wells. "See you both in the goods agent's Office at two o' clock." Jingo didn't reply. Joe nodded. Jingo's attention was called to the boiler-suited night fitter who'd looked into the messroom uninvited.

"I haven't got a repair card in for that Q6 you've just brought in? Can you do one?" the fitter asked.

"Nearly forgot. There's a few jobs. Wants a gauge glass in. We couldn't fit one cos there was only one rubber. Right big end was a bit hot at Malton. I'll put you a card in. There's quite a few jobs." Jingo had adjusted from the defendant in the interrogation to the loco driver who had won Joe's admiration for his unsung skill with the old Q6.

Joe disappeared up Sander Road walking swiftly behind Johnny Marsay's slowly-pedalled bike and discussing the state of the war. Ten minutes later he opened the back door of his home on Hastings Road and entered the darkened kitchen. The inner door to the living room opened and his mother's frail figure was framed in the doorway.

"I've been so worried about you Joe. Going to work in that state. There was blood on your pillow when I went into your bedroom this morning after you'd gone to work."

"I'm alright," said Joe, suddenly more aware of his battered face. "I'm hungry, though."

"I've got a nice meal for you. Been keeping it hot on the pan since tea-time. You're so late. What's kept you at work all this time?" His mother's questions and comments were unbroken, displaying the anxiety she had felt all day about his bruised face.

Joe had switched off his attention while he sat, with half clean hands, wolfing his dinner; his mind ranging over the opportunities for going somewhere for a short while before he would be obliged to go to bed. His Father's repeated comment broke through his veil of self-imposed silence.

"Good job you've given up boxing."

The word boxing caused a response. "What did you say Dad?"

Dad repeated. Joe responded with a puzzled, "Given up boxing?"

"That's what I said. Your Mam told me. Ridiculous being hammered like that for fun. Make more sense if you was being paid."

"You told him I was giving up boxing, Mam?"

"Yes. Two lads came earlier. They asked how you was. They said you were going to hang up your gloves. Hang up your gloves. That's how they put it. A lad called Mike and a tall lanky one."

"Yes!"

"They left sixteen shillings for your gloves. They came for the gloves because you said they were for sale for sixteen shillings."

"Where are they Mam?"

"The lads or the gloves?"

"The gloves! Mam."

"I sold them for you. They said you'd agreed on sixteen shillings. You'll be better off without them. You'll be better off playing draughts with Danny West."

"But I can't box without gloves."

"You'll have to now," chipped in Dad authoritatively.

"But I was going to make a career out of it?"

Joe went blank, and quiet. There was nothing he could do now, 'But just you wait' he thought. And he went on to recall falling out of the ring on his head and mumbling incoherently as they doused his face with water. Or was it so incoherent, didn't he recall saying, "Giving up this stupid lark."

* *

"Right, let's look at this whole problem now everybody is here." The short, quietly-spoken Castlebrough Goods Agent Mr Wilson addressed the small group of seated police and railwaymen. "I've agreed with P.C. Wells and Detective Constable Cousins to let them conduct their investigations in my office while the rest of you sit in my secretary's office." He looked around as if seeking approval. "You stay Mr Johnson, I'll ring through for anyone else." Joe loped off with the rest. He was there but he did not know why.

"We've got to be frank Mr Johnson. We think you are more involved in this than you care to admit." The civilian Detective Constable Cousins spoke pointedly to the locomotive driver who on this occasion was not uniformed.

"No." Jingo laid back at ease in his round-backed wooden chair, seemingly at pains to show that he wasn't intimidated by his persecutors.

"There's the question of your brother's handcart being present on the night you were firewatching. It was seen being pushed up the street loaded at about seven-thirty in the morning. You were seen at the bond cage about midnight. And you have, or had, a quantity of cigarettes in your locker. Do you know what I think?"

Jingo merely shook his head. The detective emphasised, "You were on firewatch duty last Thursday night. You had left your brother's handcart in the yard the previous day when you were working on the yard-shunting engine. About midnight you opened the bond cage with a key copy and you removed six cartons of cigarettes to your handcart just outside the veranda. You covered them with a sheet and took them away at seven next morning."

"I didn't. I don't know where you've got that fairy tale from."

Railway policeman Wells interrupted, "Where did you get those three packets of players that we found in your locker."

"I bought them."

"Where?"

Jingo was giving the impression that he was reluctant to cooperate. "Can't remember, I buy cigs from anywhere and anyone I can."

"Let's try another approach. What were you doing at the cage at midnight? You were seen there. A very positive identification. You were seen starting to open the door. Where did you get the key from? Was your brother involved in helping you? He's been a locksmith, we know." Questions were being fired at Jingo in quick succession.

"Which question do you want me to answer?"

"All of them."

"Yes. No. No. Yes. And, I don't know."

"You're being facetious."

"Fasee - whats - ish?"

"You not bloody-well cooperating," exasperated the detective.

"There's no need to swear." Jingo's face betrayed a little amusement.

The railway policeman intervened, giving the impression that he was trying to smooth the exchanges. "George, I've known you a long time. We've had drinks together. You know I only want to get at the truth. I've got your interests at heart as well as the railway company's."

"You are all saying that I stole those fags, and I didn't. That's not having my interests at heart."

"Did Joe Wade bring your brother's handcart to the goods yard for you?"

"Ask him. I don't know."

Joe was called in. "I borrowed Len Johnson's barrow to move some cinders from the shed to my house and to Johnny Marsay's," he answered in response to the questions. "I got it last Thursday and put three bags of cinders on it and left them on the barrow in the inward veranda. I took them round to Johnny's house next morning after fire-watching."

"What road did you go down?"

"Street," said Joe, preferring to differentiate from the use of road because roads were also sets of rails to railwaymen. "Belle Vue."

"That verifies our witness's sighting of the handcart being

pushed down there at seven a.m." the railway policeman whispered loudly to the detective and the goods agent. Joe and Jingo were able to intercept the remark.

"Might still have had the six cartons on board," said the suspicious detective.

Joe had to explain about his interest in cinders. He thought everyone knew that shed men had permission to comb the piles of cold clinkers, ash and cinders, and extract the cinders to keep the home fires burning home. "At sixpence a bag they're too good to miss," he concluded after giving the detective Johnny Marsay's address, his own and Len Johnson's address."

"You were shunting on the Gallows pilot last Thursday afternoon before your firewatching. Weren't you Mr Johnson?"

"No, I was on the shed. Working the dusthole."

"But I saw you," said the goods agent. "You were driving a side tank loco down the goods inwards side."

"Yes, at about two o'clock. But I wasn't on the late pilot. I had come across from the shed with a wagon. We put it down the goods inward for loading with a barrel of kerosene and bales of waste. It was a load the shed master was getting ready for Cudworth loco shed. We left it down at this bottom end for loading. That's when you saw me. I wasn't on the afternoon pilot. What did you think I was doing? Sizing the bond cage up so's I could bust into it?"

Jingo's responses were rather more spirited, almost a little cheeky Joe recorded.

"We're getting somewhere now," said the detective but didn't explain where they were getting. "Let's have a word with the inward checker," he concluded.

Jack Graven was the inward checker. He kept a tally of all goods unloaded on the inward side and a record of where they were sent. Jack showed all the entries he'd made on the day and the wagon number-taker's written record of the Newcastle cigarettes wagon and the Cudworth privately owned wagon that Jingo had described. Both were shown as standing at the end of the warehouse near to the bond cage.

"Who was loading and unloading with you last Thursday Jack?" asked the goods agent.

"Charlie and Wilf. You remember Mr. Wilson, it was that day Charlie trapped his thumb between the small-wheeled containers. You took him to hospital in your car."

"Yes, I do."

"Wilf had to get help to move the barrel of kerosene that Signal and Telegraph had brought over for Mr Franker's Cudworth wagon."

"Yes and I authorised two of the war prisoners to help Wilf."

"They loaded the kerosene barrel and the bales of waste onto the Cudworth wagon. Then they carried from me in the Newcastle wagon to the bond cage where Wilf was stacking."

"That Cudworth wagon's the one we took to Gascoigne Wood," broke in Joe suddenly in Jingo's direction. "The one that caught fire," he added for the benefit of the others who were listening to his intervention.

"Caught fire!" echoed two of his listeners. Joe quickly obliged with a skipped explanation about how Jingo had pushed the burning wagon clear of the explosives. "The wagon was going up properly, proper bonfire it was," he enthused. "Plenty of wood, waste, sponge cloths, oil, paraffin and cartons. Good stuff for a bonfire. I had a good look under the tarpaulin sheet when it started to burn before I ran off to tell George."

"Interesting," broke in the detective constable but it doesn't help us to know that." He showed some impatience to be proceeding but Jack Graven popped in to the exchanges.

"I didn't see any cartons in that wagon when we were putting the barrel of kerosene in?"

"They were there. A bit battered, soaking up the leaking paraffin," interrupted Joe."The only one I saw clearly said Wills of Newcastle. Old cartons with something in for Cudworth Motive Power Department."

The goods agent suddenly interjected as if a penny had dropped between his ears. "Let's break, Somebody get the kettle on. I'm going to phone the yard foreman at Gascoigne Wood about that wagon. And have a word with Mr. Franker."

The detective exchanged a blank look with the railway policeman. Their chosen scenario and corresponding detection was being overtaken, they could sense that, but no pennies were dropping between their ears. Mugs of tea appeared and the assembled group drank in silence, awaiting the return of the goods agent and hoping for a revelation that would seal the case one way or the other.

It seemed ages before the office door groaned on it's hinges to reveal the goods agent clutching a piece of paper containing his handwritten notes. "The Gascoigne Wood foreman confirms - " he paused as if deliberately to add further tension, " - that the remains of six cartons of cigarettes from Will's of Newcastle where found in the burnt out wagon."

The detective and the policeman exchanged glances, enough off an indication that the penny had dropped.

"It seems" Wilson added, with a hint of glee, now enjoying his position of momentary power, "that the Italian prisoners put them in the wrong wagon, - er, - a language problem evidently."

"Right, - er well" the detective shuffled and muttered, embarrassed now that all the wind had been taken from his sails "That solves the case for us." Jingo sat passively with his arms folded. He didn't say a word, his expression said it all. "Anyway" the detective continued as he hastily scooped his belongings together, "We are indebted to Mr George Johnson, and, of course, his mate Mr Wade, for helping us with our investigations."

"I'll have my fags back." stated Jingo firmly and with them in his possession left the goods agents Office.

" We are indebted to Mr George Johnson, blah, blah, blah," mimicked Jingo in Joe's ear as he donned his trilby and walked along the balcony from Mr Wilson's first-floor office. "That bloody tec, was after putting me inside, the Jerries at the Somme couldn't do it and that little upstart can't. You was a real champion son when the gloves were off," he grinned at Joe and flicked his ear playfully.

"The gloves are off properly now Jingo. I've sold 'em. Anyway, I'm going to become a detective." He grinned back then asked Jingo, "Do we get paid for today mate?"

"Course! A day's pay and we've only been here for an hour," he chuckled and his long ugly face cracked into an equally unattractive but jubilant smile.

1
FOR THE SECOND FRONT

"Left — LEFT - RIGHT - LEFT — Left," Mason's rhythmic bark issued marching instructions to the six uniformed locomotive cleaners marching northwards up Sander Road. In single file, with firing shovels borne like rifles on right shoulders, their heavily booted feet rang out in the gutter.

"Keep 'em up, chins back, Left — Left — Left."

"Could've done with better shovels Sarge." yelled out Frank Sutton from the back of the column.

"Best we could get, Clarkey couldn't let us have six new ones. Two's all he had. Said he'd have me goolies if I didn't bring 'em back," Joe called out. "Don't bloody lose 'em. Don't fancy me goolies hanging on a nail in Clarkey's store."

The military precision of the column started to falter as conversation commenced to dominate Mason's control. The approach of two attractive factory girls, arm in arm, was the final blow to their amateur discipline. Shovels came down, the column melted into a jostling group; caps were tipped or raised as 'ducky' and 'darling' and whistles greeted the girls."Get lost!" "Wouldn't be seen dead with you lot," were the only responses to the lad's amorous expressions.

The group rolled along the pavement in the direction of St James's Church down the dip in the road. "Two o' clock, the wedding, you said, didn't you?" Johnny Marsay called across to Joe. "What time's it now?"

Joe plucked his Grandfather's pocket watch from a trouser pocket, "Quarter to two."

"We want to hide these shovels and get into the Church before the bride comes," Mason added.

The small wedding party were assembled in the front pews awaiting the coming of the bride. Joe and his five companions filed into the back row, positioned so as to be the first to leave and retrieve their shovels and form a triumphal arch for Fireman Jack Holt and his bride Lucy.

Jack was an experienced railwayman, already appointed to the rank of full-time fireman, thirty years of age, tall and gangly, a confirmed bachelor, or so he had claimed, until Lucy had kissed him. "I'm a misogynist," he had declared for years, "Wimmen is for washing pots and their ain't no pots on the footplate. It's the loco life for me." So convinced were the listeners by his pledges to steer clear of women that when it became known that Lucy Robinson had kissed him without invitation, interest in Jack's love life had multiplied. Six months later when it became common knowledge that Jack was to marry he'd become the talk of the shed.

"She's in the club," and "It's a shotgun wedding," were the most frequent remarks amongst the loco men but these did not conceal the genuine warmth that existed for Jack who loved his work on the loco's. It was a warmth born out of his readiness to help anyone with a railway task. He would stay over after his day's work and help anyone in difficulty. News of his impending marriage and his equally joyous announcement that he was to be examined to become a locomotive driver focused more attention than usual on Jack.

When the words 'I will' had been uttered and the couple taken into the vestry for the signing Joe and his mates trooped noisily outside, donned their caps, retrieved their shovels and lined the short path from the church door.

As Jack and his bride emerged from the church the six assorted firing shovels formed an arch. A small floral spray, and a smart suit rather than a bridal gown, marked the wartime wedding. The only concessions to formal expectations were a few floral button-holes worn by guests and a handful of rice thrown for luck. The loco lads broke into a chant to accompany the- couple on their short journey beneath the arch.

"Keep a bright burning fire and plenty of water,
A good head of steam and a wide regul-a-tor,
Look after your engine, it's your power you know,
Look after Lucy, she's your power you know.
Hurrah,   Hurrah,   Hurrah."

Brief applause rewarded the lads' amateurish production and the explosions of three detonators on the rails in nearby Washbeck coal yard were heard as the coal-shunting pilot cracked them off in celebration of Jack's special day.

Jack was overjoyed by the railway dimension to his special day. "Can you lads see me in the Tavern just before three o' clock?" he asked.

"We can," replied Joe, indicating both Johnny and Frank.

"We can't," added a petulant Mason. "We've got to go back to the shed, we're working."

"Right! We'll just go up to Lucy's Mam's and then I'll come down for a drink with you lads," concluded Jack, unaware of the shadow of disappointment that drifted across Lucy's face.

* *

Sheeted and camouflaged bren-gun carriers occupied flat low-loading wagons in number one siding at Gallows Close goods yard alongside the single line to Whitby. They awaited Jim Simpson and Joe who were to take them to Selby. Joe had gone from his engine and joined Jack Holt on 8017 the W.D. saddleback shunting engine.

"How did your wedding party go Jack?" asked Joe.

"It started okay, but finished with the red flag out."

"How's that?"

"I was put in the doghouse for coming to see you lads for a drink on our wedding day. Red flag's been out ever since," grinned Jack sheepishly.

"Hope she didn't blame us Jack."

"Nah, she blamed me. I said I owed you lads a drink for the shovel arch. Good idea that. Lucy liked it too until I came to see you in the Tavern. Played hell she did. Said I was leaving her on her wedding day, didn't seem to understand."

"Wimmen's a bit like that Jack. They don't understand how a fellow's brain works."

"Yes, that's right. Especially when a fellow works on the railways. I'll have to learn her. Got to get 'em eating out of your hands as Ankler says," Jack concluded. The conversation drifted onto railway matters as Jack's engine driver climbed aboard the War Department shunting engine.

"When are you going for your driving test, Jack?" asked Joe as his eyes fell on the railway rule book that Jack had been studying prior to being joined by Joe.

"Next Friday at York I've to be at the Railway Institute for a medical with the railway doctor at ten-thirty. In the afternoon I have to go out and drive a train. Then have an examination with the locomotive inspector on rules and working."

"You're bound to be alright, aren't you. With all the time you've spent in Jim Simpson's Mutual Improvement Class."

"Yes, should be," said Jack, "but it's the medical that bothers me. I never forget my Dad going for a railway medical when I was thirteen and he failed, lost his driver's job, he did."

"It's the rules and working that bothers me," replied Joe. "There's such a lot to know." He inwardly recalled how he was awaiting the results of his own call up medical. He'd had three medicals because the doctors were not satisfied, but still no result.

"Yes but I've been at it for thirteen years now. If I don't know the job now I never will. On top of that I've been reading and learning and going to classes, 'cos I like railway work."

"I do same," returned Joe. "Whenever I'm on a job with Simpson I learn a lot from him 'cos he's keen. I'm with him today taking that string of bren carriers down to Selby. On the move for the second front we think."

"Yes Joe, probably. You can get on the move in a minute. Hull goods is just pulling away from the reception. When he's clear I'll be pulling your train down so you can leave." Jack was driving for half of the shift, gaining experience and giving his driver mate Bill Ankler a rest. A day's work on a shunting engine was very hard for a driver because of the very many heavy movements that had to be made.

Joe made off to join his engine and his mate Jim Simpson. Their thirty-five flats and bren gun carriers were pulled into position by Jack Holt on the W.D.

With the single line electric tablet in their possession they were soon on their way through the short twisting tunnel that took them beneath part of Castlebrough and onto the York line. They'd had a clear distant signal before entering the tunnel and so were able to press on in the knowledge that they had permission to run past Falsgrave signal cabin and onto the mainline.

"It's a very busy weekend this Whitsuntide. Lot of extra traffic now that the war's going in our favour. It's a good sign when people start planning their holidays," said Jim Simpson to Joe who was alongside him viewing the signals and the road ahead.

"Will it make it difficult for us to get to Selby?"

"No doubt about that, that's the reason we're being routed on Hull Road and off at Driffield to Market Weighton and Selby," said Jim. "This way will be a bit less congested than the York line. They should've let us go before that Hull Goods left in front of us."

"That was a bit daft, Jim. What do you think Control were thinking of to let the slow Hull goods leave in front of us."

"Mistake, that's what. This load of bren gun carriers is a last minute train and should've been given priority because it's special to the war effort. I asked the signalman at Gallows Close to tell Control that we should've left before Hull Goods but it didn't do any good."

"He'll be shunting Sander station now. Maybe we'll get past

him," responded Joe proud to be displaying his growing fund of railway knowledge.

"We'll soon see," said Jim as he pulled the D49's regulator wide open to get his train moving as he saw more and more of his signals fall into clear position.

The engine rode roughly and seemed exceptionally noisy. Joe felt a constant shudder and tremor vibrating through the whole of the engine as it gathered speed past the gasworks and the engine sheds. It was going to be an uncomfortable ride at speed, he was sure of that. But it was nothing to worry about he had often ridden on noisy rough engines that had shaken his intestines.

"It's a noisy engine for a D-Forty-niner, Joe."

"Yes. Can you hear a knock? Not very loud but there seems to be a knock," responded Joe.

"Sounds a bit like the big-end's knocking," shouted Jim above the growing clamour. "Sometimes they knock when they are getting worn."

The signals approaching Sander were at danger. A clear indication to Jim that the Hull Goods was in front of them. As he advanced his train slowly closer towards Sander signal cabin he told Joe that he was going to stop and ask the signalman to put the Hull goods across onto the Down Main and let them pass. "If he doesn't, and he let's him forward to shunt Cayton, Gristhorpe and Filey we'll be stuck behind him for a long time."

"I know we will. Three weeks ago I was on Hull goods and at dinnertime we were still shunting Filey," said Joe once again displaying his growing experience. "Bob Laker rang back to the shed and insisted on relief. They sent a taxi out for us. We had an eight-hour day in and we'd only done seven miles and four stations."

Simpson was successful this time. After a wait while a passenger train sped along the down line in the Castlebrough direction the Hull goods was shunted across. Then they were on their way in the direction of the small seaside resort of Filey.

The thump on the middle big-end continued to bother Jim Simpson. He wondered if the big-end key was coming loose. As they passed through the busy countryside stations of Cayton and Gristhorpe he determined to examine the big-end when they were stopped. The opportunity presented itself at Filey. The two platforms of the roofed station were quite busy, about thirty passengers and a number of four- wheeled flat barrows, stacked with dripping smelly boxes of wet fish, waited on the down platform for the next train to take them to Castlebrough. Jim and Joe hauled their thirty flat wagons and bren carriers far enough in the direction of the station's advance signal to clear the crossing gates.

As they drew slowly to a crawl Jim Simpson instructed Joe. "Drop down this side and tell me when to stop. I want the middle big-end crank to be on top front angle so that I can look at the big-end key. Can you do that Joe?"

"Of course I can. You've done that so often in the class that I'll never forget it as long as I live." Joe grinned back and quickly descended from the cab down the steps onto the lineside. "Left hand crank just below bottom front quarter," he shouted up to Jim Simpson whose head peered out waiting for the signal from Joe to bring the slow moving train to a sudden halt.

Joe joined Jim on the footplate alongside the length of the D 49's boiler and together they peered into the engine motions. "The big-end key's there but the top locking stud's missing," Jim explained. "I can't see the bottom locking stud. If that one's missing, the key would come up and likely fall out."

Jim explained a little test he wanted to apply with steam in the cylinder that would indicated the amount of slack there was between the big-end and the crank. "You'll have to operate the steam regulator and the gears but keep the brake on, we don't want the engine to move, just enough steam to take up any slack on the con-rod."

Joe dashed into the engine cab, pleased to be operating the engine controls without direct supervision. He knew exactly what he was doing, he was an avid student in the Mutual Improvement Class held usually in the station waiting room and run by both Dan West and Jim Simpson.

Jim Simpson was satisfied with his observations and joined Joe in the cab. "I'll take it easy and stop at Bridlington shed and get a fitter to look at it unless anything breaks or the key comes out before we get there."

"What'll we do if we lose the big-end key."

"At best the big-end brasses 'll come lose and we'll have to fail the engine and send back for another."

"At worst then?" asked Joe.

"At worst the big-end of the con-rod will break up and we'd be a total failure - dead stop, an' it'll be a long walk to the next signal box."

"I'll get ready for the run up hill now because the section ahead will be clearing soon." They knew that the stopping Hull passenger train from Castlebrough was just in front of them but once he'd cleared Hunmanby they wouldn't catch him up again.

Joe was right. The signal fell to clear and they set of up the four-mile bank to Speeton. Their train was not particularly heavy for the D49 which was really a large-wheeled passenger locomotive. It coped well with the exertion even though driver Simpson was driving it gingerly, keeping one ear alert for the persistent knock, much as a doctor might listen to a pulse.

The climb up the seventy foot bank was pleasant to Joe. The greens of the grasses and trees contrasted nicely with the limestone where it had been exposed by agriculture or railway cuttings. The rabbits that populated the extensive warrens just north of Hunmanby always captured Joe's attention as they dashed about in panic at the sound of the train. The engine steamed well, and, like Jim Simpson, his main awareness and concern was the steady thump that should not have been there. He wasn't really worried, more just, very interested. He didn't really care what happened to the big-end. If the engine failed it would be interesting to see how the system would rescue them and take the 'Second Front' load on to Selby.

They reached the peak just beyond Speeton without mishap. "I'm going to run down hill with a little steam in the cylinders and keep the brakes dragging," shouted Jim over the noise of the engine and across the cab to Joe. "That'll keep pressure on the con rod and maybe do more good than free-wheeling will do."

Joe understood and kept his ear on the bump of the big-end which to him didn't sound any worse. Within ten minutes they were running into the large passenger station at Bridlington. All signals were clear to proceed straight through and on towards Driffield but Jim Simpson brought his train to a halt. Joe went to the signal cabin to ask for their train to be placed in the siding close to Bridlington locomotive shed and for loco fitters to be sent out to examine the knocking big-end.

"It's a bit hot," said Ken Coates the senior engine fitter at Bridlington loco shed when he had touched the big-end gingerly. The engine was on the inspection pit in the shed and Ken was underneath taking a look. Joe and his driver Jim were alongside the engine peering between the spokes of the leading driving wheel. "Big-end key's in position but a bit loose, that's been letting the brasses play loose, not much but enough to cause friction and bumping."

"What about the two locking studs?" asked Jim through the wheels.

"The bottom one's missing, maybe sheered off. The cotter pin's still intact. That's what's stopped the key working out when the set-studs didn't hold it." The fitter then came from under the pit and continued talking. "We haven't got a spare engine for you to take. I don't know whether Castlebrough will have one."

"Can't this one be patched up?" asked Joe.

"That's what I was thinking." answered the fitter in the direction of Jim Simpson. "The white metal hasn't melted so we may be able to. I'll get an engine cleaner to cool her down with water and clean the parts then I'll see if we can get another set stud in, clean out the lubrication system and tighten the key and brasses. You two go and have a brew in the messroom."

Joe made off with his tea bottle and 'snap' and his mate Jim to the messroom, he relished a chat on railway subjects and politics. He was always stimulated by Jim's intellectual company and the inspiration he provided to be struggling for better things. With Jim he had attended Castlebrough Writers' Circle and become interested in writing poetry. Jim was the secretary of the loco shed's voluntary Mutual Improvement Class where loco men studied the theory of their craft and helped each other understand railway working. He was also an active member of the local branch of the National Union of Railwaymen to which Joe also belonged.

"The second front is being talked about a lot Jim. Do you think there's going to be one."

"Certain. It's bound to come soon because the Russians are advancing fast towards Germany. If the Yanks and the British don't get onto the continent soon it looks as if the Russians 'll take Germany and that'll make it go Communist."

"Churchill won't want that Jim. Neither will Atlee or the Labour Party."

"Don't speak about Churchill and Labour's leader, Atlee, in the same breath," came back Jim with mock anger on his face. "After the war Churchill's going to be looking for another job. That I'm sure. Labour's going to get in and bring in full employment and free national health."

Joe reverted the conversation to the second front issue. "Do you think our bren gun carriers are really for the second front?"

"Sure. They're going south. There's a lot of other arms traffic going south. Jerry 'll a know about it but they won't know when or where."

"We don't want 'em left here do we. No doubt they'll be delayed at least a day if we can't get another engine," replied Joe but then added, "Unless they repair ours."

"Yours is repaired. You can take it in a minute when Ken comes out," said the young fitter's mate who had just appeared in the doorway of the messroom.

"What yuh done?" asked Jim inquisitively.

"Refitted the key, fixed two new set-studs, and a cotter, and overhauled the lubrication system on the big-end." He approached Joe and helped himself to a swig of tea out of Joe's mug. "That's worth a drink in't it," he added cheekily.

Back at their engine Jim was being consulted by Ken Coates. "Did you get your own engine ready before you left Castlebrough?"

"No it was prepared for us by another set of men," replied Jim defensively. "Why? Was there something wrong?"

"Well I think that bottom stud's been missing for a day or two. There was too much muck in the threads for it to have just come out since leaving Castlebrough."

"Somebody's missed it when they've examined the engine. I guess that's possible because they don't usually shift often and some men forget to check them." Jim responded.

"Supposed to follow a strict routine of examination so nothing should be missed." Joe interjected knowledgeably, keen to again display his expanding acquaintance with railway practices.

"Well you can take her now," said the senior fitter. "You are going to Selby aren't you. About forty miles. You should be alright but keep an eye on that big-end for getting hot. I know you can't get at it to feel it easily when you stop, so I've put a pile of thick axle box grease on the top of the big-end. Keep looking at it when you stop. If it melts and runs down you'll know it's hot."

Jim took the advice with gratitude and left with his engine to join the train. He whistled for the siding's exit signal and soon their engine was expelling a healthy blast into the clear sky and rushing its way along the up main line in the direction of Hull. The busy little stations of Carnaby and Lockington flashed past as their camouflaged train rocked noisily on its way to Driffield where it would turn off towards Market Weighton and Selby. The engine ran noisily, the throb of the big-end could still be made out but the steady distinct knock of earlier was absent.

Jim was hoping that they might be halted at Driffield so he could examine the troublesome big-end. After Driffield they would be faced with a climb up hill for two miles to Enthorpe top. Preferably a run at the hill through Driffield was desirable but they had no choice, they had to take a quick look at the middle big-end. All signals were clear for him to run through the roof-covered station and up the hill but he slowed to a halt at the station platform.

"Joe! Stop me again with the middle big-end on front top quarter."

Joe leapt from the moving train as it was slowing to a halt. He ran forward and settled his eyes on the rotating left hand outside big-end, from it he could work out the position he needed to ensure the middle big-end was in position to be viewed. He slowed Jim to a crawl with a hand signal and then shouted "whoa." He climbed up on to the running footplate, eager to look at the problem before Jim left the cab to inspect.

"Looks alright" he shouted but that didn't stop Jim from coming forward for his own inspection. "Do you want me to lay inside Jim and touch it to see if it's hot? I could do quite easily."

"Good God No! Far too dangerous with an engine that's in traffic. If the wagons jostled while you were laid in there the engine might move and cut you in two. It's happened before. Don't let it happen to you. Never go into the engine motions or underneath unless your engine's tied down safely and no one can run into it." Clearly Jim was taken aback by Joe's apparent recklessness.

"The wagon grease is still there so it does not look hot," added Joe, keen to change the tone of reprimand that he noted.

"Yes, lets get cracking." Jim waved an acknowledgement to the signalman who still had all signals and the road gates set in the train's favour. He popped the whistle as a warning, looked back for a wave from the guard to ensure that he hadn't left the train and he was off. The beat of the exhaust and the rock of the locomotive accompanied Joe as he swung coal neatly into its position in the firebox. He was getting ready for the climb up the road to Market Weighton and Selby.

"These bren gun carriers are very heavy aren't they Jim? As heavy as many a coal train."

"Up hill like this they are. Got to remember they're armoured and tracked." He gave the engine full regulator and had the valves on thirty-five per cent cut off. The D49 held her feet and pulled uphill as confidently as any goods engine.

The roar at the chimney top and the hard blast on the fire put

Joe in mind of Jingo Johnson and how he'd flogged the Q6 after he'd fitted the 'jimmy' on the blastpipe. 'Not that there's any comparison between Jim Simpson and Jingo,' thought Joe. 'Jimmy's a more sensitive driver. Won't waste an ounce of coal or a pound of steam.'

"We're going over the Wolds now. You can see the chalk in the side of the cuttings. Quite an engineering feat getting this line up here. Lot of muck had to be moved by man and beast," Simpson informed Joe. Then he spoke of George Hudson the Railway King of the Eighteen-Forties. How Hudson had purchased Londesborough Park near Pocklington for his own private estate so he could control the land over which the rail route from York to Market Weighton would have to pass; how he'd been disgraced and died to be buried at Howsham near Selby.

For a few minutes Joe forgot his responsibility to the engine and was lost in his acquisition of knowledge which was becoming an insatiable urge in him.

"Watch the steam Joseph. We've about a mile to go yet. Then we'll be coasting down to Market Weighton."

"Are we stopping there to examine the big-end."

"We'd better stop somewhere. We'll see what the signals are telling us at Market Weighton. I don't want to stop on the mainline at Market Weighton without permission because it's quite a busy little junction of four lines."

The necessary halt took place and a quick examination indicated that the big-end was still alright. Without much trouble they ran through the gently undulating countryside and on into Selby sidings. The big-end was still in good order and when they'd collected their guard they made off in the direction of the nearest water crane and signal cabin. As yet they had no instructions for working back to Castlebrough.

"Do you know the road from Selby to York, mate?" the signalman in Selby Station box ask Jim Simpson. He'd turned from his telephone to address the question in the middle of his conversation with control.

"Yes. I've signed for it in the route book at Castlebrough."

The signalman turned to his other duties for a few moments without addressing Jim Simpson immediately.

"Did you get any instructions for us?" asked Jim.

"Yes. Go light to York and pull in near locomotive box and ask control if they need you for anything to Castlebrough. I can let you go in a minute."

Jim went back to his engine. Joe was reading a newspaper he'd collected from a nearby empty passenger train and intermittently favouring the old goods guard, whom they had to take back to Castlebrough, with his youthful wisdom on the course of the war. He had a receptive listener who had spent time in France as a railwayman during the first Great War. Joe asked him which part of France the bren gun carriers might end up in.

"The low countries, North France, Belgium through to Holland. Depends on the resistance. They're only to move infantry and light ordnance quickly. They 're not much use if they come up against armour."

"We've done our bit towards the second front," chipped in Jim. "Now we have to go light to York."

"The board's off here Jim," called out Joe peering out of the cab window.

Joe had to stand all the way now because the goods guard had claimed the fireman's seat for his own. The seniority of age was his only qualification. Light engine running on main lines was always pleasing to Joe. It meant little work for him and provided him the opportunity to view the countryside and learn what he could about the road.

The spring day, the feeling that holiday traffic was on the move again, and signals that the course of the war was changing for the better put the three in good spirits. Lineside blossom and well established crops gave a pleasing dimension to nature's picture that presented itself to the speeding D49 locomotive.

They were slowed only once as they observed a permanent way caution of twenty miles-per-hour over half-a-mile of track. Soon they were brought to a halt outside York close to the junction with the main line to London. Joe went to the telephone box at the signal post as requested by his mate for instructions. He learnt that they had to make their way into York Station and stand in a bay platform ready to double-head a Sheffield to Castlebrough express which was to be strengthened for the holiday traffic. The news thrilled Joe. He was keen and fresh. His engine was in good fettle. Why not work a non-stop express over the 42 miles to Castlebrough especially now that he'd delivered his bit for the war effort?

* * * * * *

2
CARELESS TALK

The huge York station was packed with passengers and trains. It always amazed Joe how anything moved, how anyone knew where to move to and when to stop and wait. It underlined for him what an exciting job he'd got for himself in spite of his mother's opposition. Jim knew when and where to go. He followed the path indicated by the signals and acknowledged the Locomotive Box signalman's wave, and the indication given with four fingers that he was heading for number four platform.

Joe walked around the platform, taking care to remain close to the engine. Jim checked the big-end and examined his engine for defects, He felt all the bearings for signs of running hot and oiled a few important points that were accessible. A shunter approached him and told him that the Sheffield train would be arriving in number nine in about twenty minutes for them to double head. Joe was approached by a Royal Navy seamen who was looking for information.

"You might be able to join the train we're working from platform nine to Castlebrough in twenty minutes," Joe said in answer to the seaman's concern that he had missed his connection to Castlebrough."It's from Sheffield but more carriages are being added to cope with the crowds. I'm sure you'll be able to squeeze aboard." Yes. He'd try that. He was on leave and every minute mattered.

Where had he been? Joe had asked. "It's a secret chum. Strict instructions not to talk. That's why my hat band is blank. No ship name. I'll give you a clue though." He opened the strings on his kit bag. Joe looked in. "Green bananas!" he exclaimed when he caught sight of the stalk of small green bananas. "What's the good of green bananas?"

"Here, I'll give you a few. Take them home and put them in your mother's airing cupboard. They don't want to be too hot, just warm for about a week and they'll ripen."

"Gee. Thanks I haven't seen a banana for about four years."

"Pity you're not married, if you had been she'd have been real nice to you for them."

"No I'm not married. I live in Castlebrough and work at the shed. What did you do before you joined the navy?"

"I was a lecturer in a University Language Department at Oxford. You know of Oxford?"

Jim was suitably impressed. "Yes. What language?"

"Languages," came the reply. "German, French, Russian and Greek."

"Good God!" Joe was even more impressed. "Pity you can't use them in the navy."

"I do. That's my purpose for being in the navy."

"Haben Sie ein zigaretten bitte?" It was Joe that was speaking German.

"Nien ich rauche nicht. Sprechen Sie Deutsch?"

"Nicht viel Deutsch. So little in fact that I hardly know what I'm saying," returned Joe. "We have a few German prisoners of war helping the ganger in charge of the permanent way length near our shed. I'm trying to learn from them."

"That's good. What do you do on the railway? Are you driving or firing?"

Joe was keen to explain. He felt a bit insignificant as a fireman compared with his new acquaintance who must spend radio time snooping on Third Reich secret broadcasts. "I move munitions, and freight, troop trains and of course the ordinary service trains. We've just brought a load of lightweight tanks down from the moors near Castlebrough where they've been on manoeuvres. They're going down South for the second front. You'll know more about that than I do."

"I don't really know when it's expected. That's the best kept secret of the war," replied the sailor.

"I only know what my swaddy friends say," said Joe.

"Who?"

"Swaddies, soldiers in Castlebrough. They're saying July's the grapevine day."

A call to Joe from his driver interrupted the serious conversation. "Come on Joe we'll be moving as soon as the boards are off for someone to come into Nine Platform."

"Okay." yelled Joe. Then to his sailor friend, "You'd better be off across to number nine if you're going to see if you can get on it."

"I'll have to run and I've got two kitbags and this case."

"Give me one and I'll take it on the engine."

"That will help. Can you take the bananas? Daren't risk being parted from the other two because of my documents."

"Yes. You leg it across the bridge to number nine. There'll be two engines on when we join it. See you over there."

Joe boarded his own locomotive with the kit bag containing the bananas and placed it in the fireman's locker on the end of the tender. The engine moved off without a word from Jim or the guard about the kit bag.

They were given a path on the through main and backed up on to the V2 locomotive that hauled the ten corridor coaches from Sheffield. Joe was busy preparing his fire for the journey the Castlebrough. The guard said he would 'ride back on the cushions' if there was a place for him on the train. Joe got the kit bag out of the locker ready to give to the sailor.

"What have you got there?" asked the guard.

Joe told his two companions how he was merely transporting it for the sailor. Then found himself telling them how the sailor worked in counter intelligence for the navy as an able seaman and how he'd been a lecturer in languages at Oxford University.

"Which college?" asked Jim.

"Oxford University."

"But Oxford University is a lot of colleges."

"Oh! he didn't say."

The guard showed interest in the account. "What rank was he?"

"An Able Seaman."

The guard couldn't believe it. "Working in counter intelligence? And an Oxford lecturer in languages? He'd have a high rank. Lieutenant or something high. That kid you were talking to was an able seaman."

"Yes, he said so. I'd better go and see if I can find him. If this train's full and he can't get on he'll want his kit bag. Less my bananas of course."

Six more carriages were added to the train in an effort to help clear the crowd on the platform. Joe just had time to examine the whole of the train and prepare the fire and the boiler. The train was packed with excited holiday makers. More were on the platform still seeking seats. The announcement one week ago by the Ministry of War that no extra trains would be provided to cope with Whitsuntide holiday demands had not stopped a rush of hopefuls to the seaside and the countryside. The corridors were packed and so were the two guard's vans and Joe couldn't find his sailor acquaintance.

"He'll come for it at Castlebrough," said Joe hopefully to his mate Jim but was secretly beginning to worry about the stranger and his bag. 'Surely he would have been an officer? Should've talked posh if he was an Oxford Don?' 'Why was he so interested in the Second Front and where and when it would happen?' The thoughts crowded in upon him. 'He was very interested in the train load of tanks; bren gun carriers really. A bit strange really, and he got me to tell him what was on the grapevine about a possible date for the Second Front. Sounded like 'Careless talk'. Crike! Could he be a spy? He didn't have a long coat and a broad brimmed trilby hat like they do on the pictures'.

"I'll just go and see the fireman on the V2, if you don't mind Jim. I'll find out how he's steaming. A big engine like that shouldn't have had any trouble with ten bogies."

"Yes, check his vacuum brake gauge reading and then pop into the guard's van if you've time and see what the train reading is. My reading is a good 21 inches."

Joe found that the V2 loco was steaming very badly, the fire was heavily clinkered and the right injector clack was blowing and wasting steam. The driver suspected that the superheater header had a blow on it but it couldn't be examined until they arrived at Castlebrough. Joe knew he'd have to do most of the work. He hoped their middle big-end would stand up the the extra work the big load would put on it. He walked along part of the train again and inspected the passengers but there was no sign of the lecturer-come-seaman, then he returned to his engine as departure was imminent. There was nothing to be done but leave the kit bag in his locker and hope that the sailor would appear when the train emptied at Castlebrough. He turned his attention to his immediate tasks.

All was in order. The signals fell into clear positions, the train guard signalled 'off ' with a wave of his green flag and Jim Simpson, driver on the lead engine and in charge of the brake, gave a warning blast on his engine whistle.

The twin exhaust blasts from the two engines reverberated high in the arched interior of the large station. Both driver's were exerting the engines' maximum effort and Jim Simpson was applying sand to the rails and wheels; their train was cutting across both the up and down main lines through York and nothing could pass until they were clear. They weren't expected to waste time.

The D49 blew off steam even though huge demands were being placed on it; Joe was pleased because it indicated his firebed preparations had been good. He viewed the length of the snaking train for signs of emergency as it drew out of the platform then shouted across to Jim. "All off over the bridge, distant's off as well. Give her some stick Jim we haven't done much work today."

Joe was inwardly congratulating himself on his knowledge of the road from York to Castlebrough; he knew the gradient boards, could recite all of the stations and some of the gatehouses. He knew where all of the permanent speed restrictions were. Yes, he was doing well after so short a time on the footplate. Little more than a year he'd been working on the footplate and he knew he could now take the train home if an emergency struck down his driver. On now to Clifton, Haxby, Strensal and the others. He stooped to his firing task and let his mind drift to the spy and the bananas.

'Careless talk costs lives'. 'Mum's the word'. Government exhortations to be aware of spies in the midst of wartime Britain came to mind. He'd never forgotten the tale of the First World War spies living on the bank top at Castlebrough, a chilling tale about two middle aged men who lived together as women until an early morning caller stumbled on one of them shaving. They met 'justice' in front of a firing squad so the tale concluded. 'Could the sailor be involved of similar espionage activity?' Joe wondered.

As York station receded into the distance and Haxby distant popped up onto the horizon Joe was labouring away on his Hunt class locomotive footplate keeping his fire in the best order. He eyed the chimney top and fired at just the right speed to produce the best discolourisation of gases exhausting from his firebox. The footplate rolled and rocked, the flapper plate jumped irritably, chattering away that it might trap his feet if he wasn't careful where he placed them. At speed with a load behind it, his engine was a rough rider, but Joe didn't mind riding a tiger if his boiler gauge glasses were full and a bright fire roared at him.

Joe set himself the task of spotting every signal and gatehouse, of being ready with his hand on the whistle chord at every whistle board but not to blow it. He would not usurp Jim's authority at sixty-miles per hour, it would be an irritant to any driver, even the serene tempered Jim, to have his fireman blasting on the whistle without authority. As they rounded the bend approaching Kirkham Abbey and observed the regular speed restriction of forty-five miles per hour he was seated enjoying the ride and looking out for all of the signals.

At this spot he always recalled the 'crackers' on his first express run with Bob Laker in the blackout, how he'd thrown his shovel into the firebox and acquired a rabbit in the signal cabin. As they coasted at forty-five miles per hour he saw a luckless cock pheasant take flight from the lineside woods straight into the smokebox door of his engine and be struck motionless and fall to the footplate.

He glanced back to the V2 locomotive and saw the fireman observing the same event.

'He's not having that when we get to Castlebrough. I'll bloody well see to that' Joe pledged to himself.

His mind returned to the sailorman spy. 'He wouldn't have bananas if he was a spy. They're too hard to get even for a spy. He wouldn't leave them with me on the footplate of a locomotive unless he'd planted explosives or a radio with them.' He'd seen pictures in which spies had planted bombs. The heroes in comics, which he used to read, had won battles for the Allies with bombs planted at sensitive locations. German spies must do the same things. He was beginning to feel uneasy about the kit bag with bananas, or the bomb, or the radio set. 'What the Hell's wrong with my imagination, Jim Woodley says my imagination will be the death of me. Go on don't be daft. Have a look in the bag and stop going on about it.'

Simpson blasted on the whistle as they passed through Castle Howard and shattered Joe's thoughts, then opened the regulator and the chimney top started to roar once more. The demands of the engine and not his imagination determined his actions, the shovel had to find the hands that gave it power. As he laboured, Huttons Ambo passed by and Malton signals, giving a clear run through, appeared gently in the distance and came to meet them.

Steam and water were not problems, the rough, dusty ride no unpleasant experience. The noise of the two locomotives was music to Joe's ears. 'You wouldn't even hear a bomb go off.' he mused. But suddenly he realised, 'it's no joke. A bomb going off on a train, on the engine would be a real prize for a Nazis spy. They'd sacrifice a lot of aircraft to achieve that.'

He dismissed his imagination as absurd, laboured with the shovel, operated the water injectors, looked back along the train for anything wrong, checked where they were on the line and called on his memory to forecast the next signal or speed restriction. But the 'bomb' would not go away. He turned to his locker to get his bottle of cold tea, it nestled with his jacket close to the bo- b- bananas. He felt the half-filled kit bag, he could feel the banana shapes through the cloth. Yes, they were bananas. Unless they were fake bananas. He explored the base of the kit bag which seemed soft and bulky, something there that was not banana shaped. Suddenly the engine lurched and Joe was tossed from his precarious perch on the bunker end. He staggered into the cab centre and righted himself. Jim looked at him and laughed. Joe dragged himself back to his locker and his perch. He loosened the string on the neck of the kitbag and inserted his hand. 'Yes, they feel like bananas, I think.' He broke one away and pulled it out. A small green banana, 'Yes, definitely a banana.'

"Back-board on Joe!" called out Jim as Weaverthorpe's distant signal became clear. Jim whistled, he slammed the steam regulator shut and placed the reversing screw into neutral position. "Look's like our run is stopped. Just what I expected on Whit Saturday even though supposedly no extra trains are put on."

"We've done real well Kept time all the way haven't we?" Joe had his watch out.

"You be running your fire down won't you? We'll have to leave this engine ready for traffic before we sign off." Jim paused, "What are you doing with the bananas? Let me look. Haven't seen a banana for a long time."

Joe handed it over, looked out at the road and shouted, "Board's are all off. We're being given a run." Jim responded with rapid adjustments to the reversing screw and the cocks and regulator. The blast resumed and the sixty-miles per hour speed maintained. Their wishes were answered with unbelievable ease, they passed Ganton at full speed, then Sander, then the forty-five miles per hour restricted curve. All was clear into number one platform at Castlebrough. They pulled in with a tremendous feeling of triumph as Jim Simpson braked the double-headed train to a halt close to the buffers.

"One o'clock. Forty-two miles in fifty-seven minutes non-stop. It'll be a long time before you do that again."

"Yes," Joe grinned. "I loved it. I've run the fire down wafer thin and got half a glass and a full head."

"Yes, you'll make a fireman one day yet."

Joe was about to reply when he noticed the V2 fireman, amongst the passengers, making towards the front end of Joe's engine. "The flamer's after me pheasant." he yapped and was after him as soon has he could leave the engine cab.

"That's ours mate." said Joe as the foreign loco man laid his hands on the colourful cock pheasant laid in a heap below the smokebox door at the front end of the D49.

"It's the railway company's according to the rule book. If everybody had their own," replied the stocky fireman who was about five-year's senior to Joe.

Diplomacy influenced Joe's reply. "But they didn't knock it down."

"Right. We did though."

"The four of us did." replied Joe taking what he thought was the line of least resistance that might stop the bigger fireman asserting his might to rob Joe of his right. "It belongs to the four of us." He paused, "Even though it was my engine that knocked it down."

"We'll toss for it then. Okay?"

"Okay," agreed Joe, "But we'd better see what our mates think."

Jim Simpson wasn't interested. He didn't want the pheasant. The driver of the Sheffield engine was interested, so in the cab of the V2 they each drew a coin and tossed them into the air. Joe uncovered his coin first and displayed a 'head'. The fireman got a 'tail' and the driver slowly uncovered a 'tail'.

Joe let out a triumphant cry. "Great, odd man wins. My Mam's ill in bed and a bit of pheasant 'll do her the world of good." He picked the pheasant up by its neck.

"Odd man wins. What you mean? Odd man out more like." said the Sheffield fireman.

"Course not. Not in this part of Yorkshire. We always toss, odd man out wins. I've got some bananas I'd like you to have. If you like bananas? I won't be a minute."

The bananas had emerged in Joe's conversation as a diversion. "Okay," replied the driver but the fireman sullenly displayed his dissatisfaction.

The image of the sailor appeared alongside the bananas in Joe's mind as did the thought, 'Crike what if the sailor's been for the kit bag while I've been here.' He was out of the cab quickly making his escape with the pheasant.

"Anybody been for the kitbag, Jim?" he asked as he climbed into the cab.

"No, not for the bag. The shunter's been. He wants us to loose off and let the Sheffield man take the train down to Gas Down. You'd better do that now."

The bananas had to wait. Joe had to ease himself down between the two engines and the platform and uncouple his engine from the V2 before he could deal with the bananas.

Back in the cab he found the Sheffield fireman waiting for him. The stocky fellow's eyes were possessively placed on the pheasant laid out on Joe's seat. Joe extracted the kit bag from the locker and removed the stalk of bananas. "There," he said, "a dozen bananas for you, and a dozen for your mate." They were taken by the sullen figure without comment or thanks, clearly he thought he was getting his cut in some enterprise but he wasn't satisfied with his allocation.

"Were they yours to give away, Joe?" Jim asked with a half-serious face when the Sheffield fireman had departed.

"Who else's?" asked Joe confidently.

"That officer seaman," returned Jim.

"But he isn't here. Maybe he never intended joining our train."

"What would he do that for when he'd given you his bag?"

"I'm not sure. But I thought he might be a German spy."

Jim laughed out aloud, "A German spy! Whatever made you think that?"

"He questioned me so closely about troop movements and munitions. And whether I'd heard anything about when the second front was being launched. I thought there was something fishy. That's why I offered to take one of his bags. Thought I could examine it before we got to Castlebrough and he came for it."

"Did you find anything?"

"I haven't had time to look. I'll look now." Joe put his hand and arm to the bottom the of the kit bag and pulled out newspapers and typewritten sheets which were crumpled in the bottom. "That's a Berlin newspaper. Look, dated 21st of some month in 1938. These are typewritten notes in German Looks as if I could have been right about him."

An engine whistle popped and the Sheffield locomotive started to back the long empty train out of the platform. When it was clear he and Joe got their path to the shed.

"What do you think I'd better do with them Bill?" Joe was asking Bill Clarke as he, with a number of shed men and loco men, examined the newspapers and documents.

"I'll give them to Franker and he'll give them to the police for examination. Course, they might want to interview you. With a bit of luck you'll get a medal from the King," Bill Clarke clipped Joe's ear playfully.

The papers were placed in the kit bag and left with chargeman Clarke. Joe then set off for his engine where he had left the remaining bananas and the pheasant and prepared to sneak off home with them.

* * * * * *

3
UNWELCOME RESULTS

The post brought some unwelcome news for Joe on the Tuesday after the Whitsuntide weekend. "From the Castlebrough Medical Board, for you Joe," said Joe's Father to him as he entered the living room at home just before breakfast. "I've opened it because I'm going to work and I wanted to know what they wanted with you. Look on it as good news." He handed an open envelope to Joe.

Heavy with sleep, even though he'd just had a cold wash, Joe responded slowly, "Ta." What could be good news for him he wondered? as he sat down at the square dining table, that now replaced the Morrison table air-raid shelter. From the envelope he withdrew a printed green card which notified him the result of his recent conscription medical. 'My three medicals' he thought recalling how he'd been on three occasions for the standard medical examination at Unity House including a three-hour visit to the local hospital.

"Grade Four," burst out Joe. "I've been excused call up on the grounds of my medical grading. Blooming cheek. Even Mam said I'd be A1 grade because I was the strongest. Tim went into the R.A.F. A1 and I'm bigger and fitter than he is. It don't say why I'm grade four. Am I blind or blooming deaf?"

"You're better off not going." His Mother's voice interrupted his thoughts. "Anyway even if you'd been A1 they wouldn't have taken you from the railways because it's a reserved occupation." She sounded almost triumphant.

He recalled how he'd applied to join the Royal Naval Boy's Service when he was fourteen but his Father had said, "You can fill the forms in if you like but I'm not going to give my consent." They had the same showdown when he applied to join the Boy's Army Service a year later. He felt now that he would never get to sail the ocean waves, fight in foreign lands, or fly to the stars, 'Per Ardua Ad Astra', at the state's expense.

He was morose, almost sullen but he knew it wasn't his Mam's fault. He was forced into conversation. His younger brother Luke was breakfasting with him before setting off to his job as a store assistant in a local Cooperative shop.

"What did they say was the matter with you Joe?" asked Luke and then added, "They say they take anyone now unless they are very ill or handicapped. Grade Four's a bit low isn't it?"

"They didn't say. They don't tell anyone the reasons, they say." replied Joe glumly.

"But the railway doctor has passed you fit twice since Mr. Bowman got you a job as a Porter," said Emily Wade sympathetically.

Joe cheered up, "Course he has. I must be alright."

"Why did they send you to the hospital for tests? Was it because you couldn't cough?" Luke light heartedly added the second question.

"All I know," Joe addressed his Mother, "When they tested my water a white fluffy thing formed in the test tube. Like a snow flake."

"Was it sugar?" his Mother asked.

"He doesn't know. He didn't taste it. Did you Joe?" Luke couldn't miss the opportunity to try to raise a laugh.

Joe ignored the repartee. "I heard the doctor say to his clerk, 'albumen'. Or something like that I don't know what that is."

"Can't you ask the railway doctor?" Joe's Mother asked and then added, "After all you might not be fit enough for the railways."

Joe shuddered inwardly. Every locomotiveman feared failing his medical and having to give up his job. "I don't have to tell the railways and I'm not going to. I'm just telling everybody that I'm not in the forces because I'm on a reserved occupation and not allowed to join. Because that is the truth."

Joe did not tell anyone at work about his medical grading. When Mr Franker asked to see him in his office that afternoon when he signed on at 3pm for the last train Castlebrough to Whitby at 4.35pm he suspected that he might be asked about his medical but he was wrong. "Mr Franker is in there with railway policeman Maurice Wells in the inner office," Douglas Firth, the shed master's clerk informed Joe as he entered the shed office. Jack Holt was present collecting a railway travel warrant for his journey to York on the coming Thursday for his driving test. They exchanged a few words.

"Will you be at the mutual improvement class on Sunday Joe?" asked Jack.

"Intend to, if I'm not working. You'll be passed-out by then. Will you be there?"

"Hope so. You seeing the boss?"

"He asked to see me. Don't know about what. Hope he wont be long, I'm on back-turn Whitby. Pity he's got the copper with him. I'll have to wait."

Joe didn't have to wait. The inner office door opened and Mr Franker looked out and waved Joe forward. Joe was surprised to be in the office with Franker and the Policeman Wells whom he hadn't seen since the investigation into the missing cigarettes.

"Sit down Joe." After a suitable pause in which Joe became seated and the shed master collected some papers he said, "I just want to know, and P.C. Wells wants to know, about these German papers." He indicated the papers with a brief flourish.

"Yes," responded Joe cautiously. 'Why is Wells here?' Joe thought suspiciously. He hadn't forgotten how the police had so readily accused Jingo.

"Where did you get those German papers that you left with Bill Clarke last Saturday?" Franker asked.

"Off a sailor," Joe answered cautiously. He was alert to the need not to incriminate himself.

"Where?"

"At York."

"Did he just give them to you?"

"Yes"

"He must have said something. Where did you meet him?"

"He was a passenger at York. He was going to get on our train."

"Did you know him?"

"No."

"Can't you say anything more than 'Yes' or 'No'?"

"Yes."

"This is getting boring, Joe."

"Yes."

"Can't you tell me how you met him and how the hell he gave you his papers."

Joe was going to say 'Yes' but he bit his tongue and reminded himself that he was talking to his shed master who had the power to dismiss him. So he thought for a few seconds. "We were stood on platform four at York waiting to double-head the train from Sheffield. He'd missed his own train. I told him where our train was and he gave me the kitbag with bananas in it. He was going to collect the kitbag when he joined our train on platform nine but for some reason he did not turn up?"

"Did he mention anything to do with Germany?"

"No." Joe was going to let it go at that but it occurred to him that Franker wouldn't appreciate a return to the 'Yes', 'No' exchanges. "He could speak German. He said that he was a lecturer in German language at Oxford University before the war, before he became an officer in the navy deciphering German radio messages."

"But you thought he might be a spy, or so you told Bill Clarke."

"I just wondered with him speaking German so well and asking questions about when I thought the second front might be coming."

"But you told John Marsay that you suspected that he had planted a bomb on the engine."

"No I didn't. Yes I did. But I didn't mean it like that," Joe stammered on.

"Well." Franker waited.

"What I meant was that I got to thinking it were funny him giving me his kit bag and then never coming back for it. I just thought 'What if he'd planted a bomb in the kit bag.' That's why I looked in the bag to see what was in it."

"You've got a fertile imagination haven't you?"

"Have I?"

"What happened to the bananas? He wants them back."

"Oh! good gracious me," Joe answered. "He wants them back!"

"Yes. Where are they?"

"He gave them to me. Well he gave me some. I shared them out with other railwaymen."

"Why?" came back Franker with an obvious insistency.

"They would have gone rotten. There's a war on. Don't you know? Bananas is food. What did you expect me to do?" Joe was fighting back. Attack is the best form of defence he'd heard someone say.

Maurice Wells had been listening and saying nothing but he ended his silence. "Well, he wants them back. We know who he is. We were able to trace him through those papers, back to Oxford and his navy posting."

"Was he a spy?" Joe asked the question incredulously.

"No, he's a serviceman home on leave in Filey."

"What about the papers?" asked Joe

"Those papers," answered Policeman Wells, "they are in German. The screwed up newspapers are Berlin daily newspapers dated before the war, in 1938 in fact. The typewritten sheets are worksheets in German language. They are headed, 'Department of Languages at Logan Green College.' They are just old papers used in somebody's language classes. The police aren't interested in them but you did right to hand them in."

"Yes, I knew," said Joe with a feeling of confidence returning, "The 'Railway Rule Book' says that railway servants must hand in anything they find on railway property. So I handed it in."

"What about the bananas?" continued Maurice Wells.

"Oh! he gave them to me. I didn't find them. And I shared them out with other railwaymen."

"Yes, the rule doesn't apply to them if they were given. It applies to things lost or laid about, wood, coal, rabbit's and er, pheasants. Anything you might think had no owner," added Franker emphatically.

Joe turned and addressed his shed master, "I'll have to go now Mr Franker I'm on the late turn Middlesbrough with Jim Simpson and I've got to prepare the engine yet."

"Okay son, remember what I said to you when you joined us. Keep out of trouble."

"Yes, keep out of trouble," added P.C. Wells. "This is the second time we've met formally. Don't want a third time. Do we?"

Joe left with the thoughts, 'Wonder why the beggar mentioned 'pheasants'. Somebody been talking? He didn't ask about my medical though, I'm glad about that.'

* *

The Sunday morning mutual improvement class was poorly attended. No one expected a good attendance because work was placing great demands on the time and energy of all railwaymen, especially locomotivemen. Sundays at Castlebrough loco were almost as busy as during the week, only the nature of trains was different. Sundays were used for track-maintenance trains, and other work that couldn't be done during the week, and of course there were the passenger services that were almost as numerous as on weekdays.

"Not a very suitable venue for a class," said Jim Simpson as the six enthusiasts agreed to start. "But if Mr Franker hadn't given us his office to meet in we would not be meeting because we couldn't find anywhere else."

"It'll do for us six," said Frank Sutton.

"That's what I thought," returned Jim Simpson. "And I wanted us to meet because the Railway Institute had this working model of Stephenson's Link motions and valve gear booked out to us this weekend and it was too good a chance to miss."

"I've only got until dinner-time," said Joe as they all noted the three-foot large working model of pistons, valves, eccentrics and cranks on Franker's desk.

"We'll spend an hour on this for all of us and then do some work on Rule 55 for the cleaners and passed cleaners like Joe and Frank.

"Where's Jack? Jack Holt," asked Frank? "He's always keen. Usually here isn't he."

"He's married now. Maybe he can't get out of bed," grinned Mason.

"More like she won't let him come," guffawed young Meecher the most recent addition to the cleaning staff.

"He went to York on Thursday for his passed fireman examination," added Joe. "Maybe he feels like a rest from studying now he's passed."

"He passed did he?" asked the class secretary Jim Simpson.

"I don't know, I haven't seen him. He's so knowledgeable that he's bound to pass isn't he?"

They started their examination of the hand-working model. Each taking turns to hand crank it into positions asked for by Jim Simpson.

"Place it in foregear Joe with the right hand valve lead port on cut off to expansion." Joe did. Proud and pleased to win Jim's approval. The door to the outer office opened as someone else came to join the class. It proved to be Jack Holt and the class continued after an exchange greetings. Jim continued. "Knowledge of motion positions is crucial if you're going to pass as a driver. Isn't it Jack?" Jack nodded authoritatively. "Did you get many questions on the motions and related questions."

"Some. You know what locomotive inspector Graven's like. He's a stickler on mechanical theory."

"As long as you pleased him," smiled Jim. "You did didn't you? Was he satisfied with your answers?"

"Yes," said Jack glumly. He made Joe think, 'What's a matter with him? Isn't married life suiting him?'

"What about your driving test? Where did you go?"

"York to Starbeck with a stopping train and back. Had a Hunt class going up and a D20 coming back."

"Two engines you were familiar with. You must have had a very good day?"

Jack was biting both lips, his face betraying some emotion. The group's attention focussed on him. Was it his marriage? Or had something awful happened to him? A crash maybe.

Jack answered their unspoken questions. "I failed my medical?"
It was as if grief had struck the group. As if a death had been announced. Thirty year old Jack was almost on the verge of tears. His first love would to be taken away from him, he would never fire or drive a locomotive again if the railway doctor had failed him.

Jim spoke, "Can't you work on local work at the shed and on the pilots?"

"No, it's my eyesight, I'm colour blind. I can't even be a guard, or a signalman, just a shed labourer."

"What kind of colour test did you do?" asked Jim.

"The Imayara book test. The one where you can see figures and shapes in coloured discs. And a practical test with the station signals. I complained but another doctor was brought in and he failed me also. I'm developing short sight as well. I'll have to wear glasses."

Responses were sympathetic and helpful. "Get on to the union, they'll help." "Ask for another test." "Can't you go to Pilmoor? Men get through the Pilmoor test sometimes after being failed." No one asked what job he wanted to do. They knew that. He wanted to be a locomotiveman.

He answered the obvious unspoken question 'What are you going to do?' "I've been offered a job in Lucy's brother's firm at Leeds. They have a large boiler section, engineering shop and water purifying plant, they've asked me to be the foreman, on good money, better than here. Lucy wants me to go. Looks as though I've no choice. It's tough having to give this job up. Funny isn't it. I came from Neville Hill shed to be promoted to fireman at Castlebrough." He would have continued talking but the others broke into his sadness.

"Let's all go and have drink in the tavern. Drowned our sorrows." said Frank.

"Only those over eighteen if I'm going," said town councillor Jim Simpson.

"We'll drink shandies seeing you're with us Jim." Joe led the chorus from the younger members.

The group wandered up Sander Road towards the 'Railway Tavern', not as cheerful as they would have been if they had been celebrating Jack's promotion to part-time driver but chattering away. The drift of their conversation added up to commiseration with Jack Holt. Joe felt a deep sense of empathy with Jack because of his own disappointing medical examination result. 'There but for the grace of God go I,' he thought, 'Suppose I'll never get in into the forces and fight the Germans. Best stick to the railway and keep quiet about medicals.' He'd done his best for the war effort, his bit for Britain. He'd delivered the bren gun carriers, he'd spotted a suspected spy and importantly he'd avoided 'careless talk'. Despite Jack's disappointment, that Joe shared, he swelled with a modest sense of achievement, his contribution to the coming of the second front was only on home territory and not at the front line, 'But,' his thoughts continued, 'perhaps its better that way, like me Mam says.'

Mason broke into his thoughts. "Who's next in line to be promoted fireman in Jack's place. Is it you Harry?"

"Dead men's shoes. That's how we get promoted," Joe said as Harry Gibson started his reply.

1
THE ONE LEGGED FIREMAN

"You're going to eat already, are you?"

Joe grinned in return, "I'm always hungry. Anyway, seven a.m. isn't a bad time to be eating." He opened his metal food tin which was a standard box carried by most locomen.

"But it's dinner pack not breakfast pack. What are you going eat at Hull when I'm having my pack?" Driver Jerry House asked his fireman.

"Dunno."

"What you got, anything nice?"

"Cheese sandwiches and two whole tomatoes. First time I've had whole tomatoes to eat like apples. My Mam's always sliced them before. I feel like eating now before we set off to Hull."

"You'll give yourself indigestion firing on a full stomach. We set off at seven-twenty-five. And this run is quite hard on a fireman."

A voice from outside the cab interrupted them. Their locomotive stood attached to nine old non-corridor passenger coaches on platform five. "Morning Jerry." The train guard looked into the engine cab. "I've got two chaps here who'd like to look aboard if that's alright with you?"

The first young man aboard, in khaki uniform and forage cab, leaned out towards his companion and collected two crutches that were being handed up. A big fellow with only one leg hauled himself up and hopped into the cab. The guard followed and the cab became a little crowded.

"Thanks pal," said the big fellow to the driver as he hauled himself up onto Joe's bench seat.

"These lads have a special reason for remembering this platform and a Hull train in particular." The guard looked towards the two visitors. "They were involved in that pile up here last August. Weren't you?"

"Yes, I lost my leg and some other bits. And some mates. John here, was injured too. Bit less seriously than me."

"Yes, You were on top of me, shielding me. You took some of what I should've had."

Joe was excited. "Last August, I was here too, in this platform. I remember it clearly, the train had its first two coaches full of soldiers going to Hull at about 11 o'clock and a Hull train coming into Castlebrough, with a D20 loco and Brid men on board ran into it. Their view was obscured by the station cabin." Joe had been there as a Lad Parcels Porter before he'd become a locoman. "Four killed and thirty-one injured. The signalman ....," Joe paused.

"Did you see me and John, trapped between the walls of the sixth compartment in?" Joe's head shook. "Did you see my mate Charlie Wright. Pinned up near the chimney? He bought it poor Charlie did."

"Yeh, I remember him. It was tragic. Buried to the waist up near the chimney he was. Two chaps laid alongside him, giving him smokes, they was, and talking to him. Poor lad, he bought it did he?"

The two soldiers were happy to be talking to someone who had witnessed and been involved in the crash. The minutes flashed by and Jerry announced that they'd have to be on their way to Hull in five minutes.

"Sorry but this is important to us. Especially to Mick who was very badly injured," said John the uniformed soldier.

"I'd like more time to talk to you, son," added Mick the injured soldier in civvy clothing.

"We have to go in four minutes. Can't you ride a bit of the way with us?" Joe asked of the pair without thought for the consequences and as if he had the right to issue invitations.

"Of course I can. It'd be a real favour. Help me to get over the shock? I was a fireman for a couple of month's at Dairycoates when the war broke out but I was in the Territorials and got called up."

"Can't have someone on the footplate whose in army uniform," said Jerry showing concern.

"I'm not in uniform," said Mick.

"He is," returned Jerry.

"But I'm getting off," answered the uniformed soldier.

"You put my cap and jacket on," said Joe handing over his cap to Mick.

"But I can't have a member of public on - -," started Jerry.

"Technically I'm still a railway servant. My job is reserved for me when I get discharged from the army."

Jerry was about to say, 'You can't be a fireman with one leg,' but withheld the remark. The one legged 'soldier' was being helped into Joe's jacket as his mate John disappeared with the crutches.

Quietly spoken, flat-capped Jerry was overwhelmed by the

speed of the decisions taken around him. The guard's whistle
sounded and the signals fell to clear. Jerry pulled on the hanging
regulator handle of the D49 locomotive, and popped his engine
whistle. The snifter valve in the superheater header clacked shut as
steam flowed to the cylinders and the train heaved out of platform
five.

Joe couldn't wait to talk to their passenger. "Last August 11th,
I was over there on the next platform loading the Pickering
sentinel rail car."

"That's right. I remember seeing that, green it was and there
was two lasses waving to us. Most of us was shouting and whistling
as if we'd never seen a lass before. Suddenly there was hell of a
bang, we all turned over and the walls came in."

"Yes," replied Joe energetically, "I saw the train with the D20
locomotive come round station cabin and plough into your train
full of soldiers. Bloody time stood still it did, it was as if I was
looking at a photograph, nobody was moving. I remember
shouting, 'help the poor buggers' to the Pickering driver stood
near me. All of a sudden people started rushing about."

"Keep your head in Mister," interrupted Jerry, aiming his order
at the soldier garbed in Joe's cap and jacket. "I don't want anyone
at the shed seeing that I've got a passenger." Then to Joe, "You
keep a look out when you're not firing. Don't be gassing and miss
anything."

"Okay Jerry," acknowledged Joe but immediately resumed his
animated conversation with Mick. "Yes, we started pulling the
sides and doors off to get at you lads inside, sandwiched up
between the telescoped compartment walls. Some of us were
putting lighted fags into the mouths of those we could reach."

Jerry's train was scheduled to stop at every station between
Castlebrough and Hull, a forty-seven mile journey with eighteen
stops taking one hour and forty-five minutes. It kept Joe busy at
his shovel but it didn't stop him spending a lot of time with his
'guest' exploring their joint memories. He told Mick everything he
could recall from that day and the result of the subsequent
enquiry.

"I ran up to the signal box to phone for ambulances. John
Smith, the signalman was stood completely still with a hand on a
signal lever. I shouted, 'Has anybody phoned for ambulances,
John?' He turned and replied 'Yes', but tears were running down
his cheeks. 'Has anybody been killed? Joe,' he asked. Often I had
my sandwiches up in his cabin. Real nice bloke, told me lots

about how the signal box worked."

Joe had to paused for breath because he was getting excited, then he continued his account of the tragedy for Mick. "I said, no, course not, John. There's nobody killed. It will be alright. I put my arms around him. He said that he'd mistaken the bell signal to mean that the light engine was coming and he'd turned Hull passenger train into five. Poor John, easy mistake to make. He'd been a signalman for thirty-three years and never made a mistake. That was said at the inquest and the inquiry."

Joe told his tale to the victim of the crash as they made their way through Sander, Cayton, Gristhorpe and Filey, stopping at each place to leave or collect parcels, newspapers and passengers.

"But there were four soldiers killed," said Mick. "Didn't you know?"

"When I was in the cabin I didn't know how many but I knew at least one had been killed. I said no one had been killed to comfort him. He was still having to work his cabin. I'd been with one soldier hanging out of the wreckage who died while three of us were trying to help him. I couldn't tell that to John, could I?"

At Gristhorpe the station master forewarned Jerry House that he would have to uncouple his engine at Filey and pick up a horsebox from the cattle dock to take to Hull.

"Will I have to loose off?" Joe asked of his driver.

"No a porter should uncouple and couple."

The soldier, seated in Joe's lookout place, used the opportunity of this discussion to express his thanks to Jerry at being given the opportunity to ride on a loco again. "I fired on the goods from Hull to Castlebrough a few times. This is a real treat. It's likely I'll never get on the footplate ever again even when I get a leg fitted."

"Remember Douglas Bader. He got back to flying and he'd lost both legs," added Joe optimistically. "Anyway, back to the crash. At the enquiry John Smith accepted the whole blame. He was devastated. Said he simply made a mistake and pulled the wrong signal off. He had a Hull train coming into Castlebrough and a light engine coming up to work your Hull train out of five platform. He mistook the passenger train for the light engine and turned it into your train."

"Whatever happened to him afterwards?"

"He's finished with signalling. He'd been ill off work for a long time. He's been back at work as a ticket collector. Such a nice fellow. Real popular with everyone. He'd a railway career without a blemish it was said at the enquiry?"

At Filey, to pick up the horsebox, they had to go into the siding near the small gasworks. That's what Joe took it to be, but it was so primitive he wasn't sure whether it was a gasworks or a coking plant. It fascinated him to see blazing red hot coals being dropped mechanically into a long-handled barrow which one man then pushed beneath a large extinguishing shower. The dust and stink were incredible. The extinguished coke was deposited to cool off and dry.

Joe wondered what the horse in the box would have made of the fiery scene if it had been loaded at the same time. He took the opportunity to visit the horse in the box before they left Filey. It was for Beverley races. He got its name, 'Second Front', and judgment of its form from the stable lad who accompanied it. He promised himself to back it next day when it ran in the three o'clock. He'd never forgotten Bill Ankler cleaning up on the tip they'd picked up when they were derailed at Heslerton.

The climb up the bank from Filey to Hunmanby and Speeton was without incident except for the harder work that it imposed on the bareheaded Joe. The run down hill on the long straight bank to Bempton, Flamborough and Bridlington was an adequate and pleasing return. The train sped down the Yorkshire Wolds close to where they joined the sea to form the spectacular cliffs at Flamborough and Bempton.

Mick continued to express his appreciation of the chance to ride on a loco on his home stretch. Jerry hadn't the heart to press for him to leave at Bridlington, or even reprimand Joe for issuing the invitation. The morning June sunshine and nature's way of painting everywhere in green of all shades helped to sooth all irritations. They ran on time through all stations from Bridlington onwards to Beverley, where in the covered station, Joe took the opportunity to visit the horse 'Second Front' pat her nose for luck and say, "Do your best old girl, won't you?" He had to uncouple the horse-box and shunt it into the little nearby siding and then reconnect to his own train because there was no local staff available.

When the train hauled slowly into Paragon station at Hull Joe knew his task was to uncouple and run into the next platform by an adjoining spur to allow escape to the locomotive shed at Botanic Gardens. First he wanted to help Mick to leave the engine, if possible without too much fuss, as it was a little bit unusual to witness a one-legged man climbing from the cab of a working locomotive.

"I'll help you down Mick," came a voice from behind Joe as he prepared to help Mick back out through the cab doorway on his one leg. Joe and Mick both turned and were faced by two uniformed locomotive men.

"Hello old mate how yuh doing," Mick grinned. "Just let me do it myself. It's amazing how you manage when you've lost something you thought you couldn't do without." His one leg and arms lowered him successfully, unaided from the engine cab onto the platform. His soldier friend was at hand with the crutches. "My old mate at Dairycoates shed." He addressed the locoman with evident pleasure. "You haven't seen me since this accident have you." Their hands clasped warmly and long. "I had a long time in Castlebrough Hospital, then a services hospital and finally Pinderfields."

"What are you doing on here, Mick?"

"Went up to Castlebrough with my oppo to see the place where the crash happened. Joe here was at the crash and we've been exchanging notes. Then Joe and his mate let me come back on the footplate. It's been great to feel the front-end wheels under me. What you doing?"

"Just going to beg a lift to Botanic Shed on here," he said indicating Joe's loco. "We're just picking up two engines for repair at Dairycoates."

"We'll have to be off when I've uncoupled," said Joe as he prepared to turn away. "Glad to have met you Mick. See you again sometime." Mick shook Joe's hand warmly. The engine passed through the adjoining spur on to the neighbouring empty platform and proceeded tender-first to Botanic Gardens Locomotive Shed.

* * * * * *

2
WHEN THERE'S A CRASH

"That crash you was talking about reminds me of the head-on collision between two passenger trains from Castlebrough and Hornsea in 1927." Joe heard the driver friend of Mick say as they were travelling to Botanic shed and talking about Mick and his experience at Castlebrough.

"I do too. I was nearby at Botanic at the time," said Jerry. Joe made a mental note to pursue that later with Jerry once they had turned and watered their engine. But other concerns were to beat Joe to the question he was saving for Jerry. They were to work the ten-forty-five stopping passenger train back to Castlebrough so they had adequate time before ringing out for permission to travel light-engine back to Paragon passenger station.

"This isn't mine," Jerry House said in bewilderment as he opened his snap tin in preparation to eat. Joe looked on having consumed all his sandwiches at Castlebrough and still having an appetite for more. Jerry went back to the locker at the coal tender and fished about in the depths and came up with an identical tin. "This is mine. J.H. is scratched on the lid." He seated himself and suddenly expressed in surprise. "But it's empty Joe. I'm sure I didn't bring an empty tin." He opened the first tin again. "This is full. Where's your tin Joe?"

"It'll be in the locker," returned Joe and proceeded to search in the locker. "No it isn't here," he said as he turned towards Jerry. "That empty one, let me look at it ? Yes, it's your tin, it's empty."

"Yes," grumbled the mild mannered Jerry, "and your tin is still full. You've eaten mine. When you were eating at Castlebrough this morning and saying how good it was you were eating mine."

Joe couldn't bring himself to reply immediately. He examined the two identical tins, identical but for one feature, J.H. was scratched faintly on the lid of the empty one. He was desperately seeking another explanation but he was beginning to recognise that he had indeed sat down in front of Jerry and eaten Jerry's food.

"Gee! I'm sorry Jerry. I remember saying that my Mam usually sliced the tomatoes in my pack but this time they were whole like oranges. What's in my tin?"

Jerry passed the tin across the cab with a slight show of irritability. "You look, it's your tin."

Was Jerry getting ready to express his anger? Or was he just peeved? Joe didn't know but waited expectantly as he took the tin.

"Cheese and tomato sandwiches. The tomatoes are sliced in the sandwiches. I was a bit surprised when I saw whole tomatoes in my tin, er, the other tin, your tin I mean." He was surprised by Jerry's quiet expression of annoyance. 'Thank God, I'm not with Bill Ankler or Jingo. They'd have blasted me and eaten my sandwiches,' Joe thought. Then he said "You eat my sandwiches Jerry. I'm ever so sorry for eating yours. It was an honest mistake. Here eat mine. I'm full."

"No, I'm alright I'll manage." Jerry's reply perplexed Joe. It was only fair that Jerry should eat Joe's sandwiches. Joe kept offering. Jerry kept refusing. "No, you eat them. It'd be a pity to throw them away." concluded Jerry firmly.

The mild mannered Jerry House was a real puzzle to Joe. Jerry had talked to Joe about the first Great War in which he'd been an infantry man. Joe learnt something of Jerry's experiences, nothing that was boastful, nothing that was complaining, just descriptions of the sufferings of others. The simplest unheroic story that was burnt into Joe's memory was of an infantry bayonet charge through the blasted woods at the battles of Ypres, through mud and the long-still dead with staring eyes and flies, through the leafless shattered trees and the screaming, through the shell fire and the stuttering of machine-gun fire.

This image of Jerry did not marry up to the timid quiet figure that arrived at work one hour before he was due and left for home at least an hour after his booking off time. According to the malicious jesting within the shed community, Jerry was scared of his wife and preferred to spend his time at work rather than at home with his wife. They were wrong Jerry was very conscientious, very principled and kind, not ambitious or pushy. Now he was insisting that Joe eat the sandwiches and let him go without food all day.

Silence reigned. Joe sat close to the full tin. Jerry kept punctuating the silence with, "You eat your food Joe." But Joe was too embarrassed. He was relieved when an old driver, known to Jerry, joined them requesting a lift on their engine to Paragon Station. It was a welcome intervention for Joe.

"Hello Jerry. Just eating are you?" asked the elderly visitor.

"He is," replied Jerry.

"Don't let me interrupt you. I'm just going to Paragon to conduct a Halifax express in from Brough."

"You can't interrupt Joe when he's eating," said Jerry. "He eats everything he can lay his hands on. Don't you?"

"Yes," muttered Joe and decided the best course for him was to cease protesting and eat Jerry's sandwiches. With a full mouth he tried to change the course of the conversation. "You were saying, Jerry, at Paragon, that you were here in 1927 when a Hornsea express ran head-on into an express to Castlebrough." He was successful, both his listeners responded with interest.

"I remember that. The Valentine's Day crash, fourteenth of February 1927. Just over there, past the signal cabin. Twelve killed," responded their passenger.

"That's the one. I was a passed fireman at Botanic Shed. Terrible smash," said Jerry. "We all rushed across from Botanic to help."

"I was just backing up with an old F class into six platform to take a stopping passenger to Barnsley," broke in the Botanic driver. "You never forget a sight like that as long as you live. Head on, on the same line."

Jerry added. "The wall between the railway and the workhouse infirmary had to be pulled down to get the injured into hospital. Nurses were climbing over the wall on ladders to get to the train. That was quite a sight to see the nurses in brilliant white uniforms and flowing head garb climbing over the wall and rushing to the two trains."

Joe, still champing away at the sandwiches which Jerry should be eating, interjected excitedly. "How could a head-on collision have happened. Did the drivers make a mistake?"

Jerry and the visitor jointly uttered, "No." Then the visitor continued, "It was the fault of the signalman er, the signalmen, I should say, because there were three operating Park Street signal cabin that morning. I remember it well because sixty-year old George Clark took the blame. He pulled points lever 95 instead of 96. He denied it. Blamed the electro-pneumatic system that operated the points."

Joe was incredulous. "Just one points lever, pulled wrong, caused a head on collision."

"Million-to-one chance that it could happen the inquiry said." Jerry added.

The visiting driver came back straight away, "Not quite as simple as just pulling that one lever. He just happened to pull it during a two second period when it was not locked. Just think of that, 'tick-tock'. The time it takes to say 'tick-tock'. That's the time he had to make the mistake. If he'd pulled just a fraction later it wouldn't have pulled over, it would have been locked by the passage of the train."

"You know a lot about this Mister," said Joe.

"Yes. Me name's Chalky White. Jerry here knows me. We both worked here at Botanic at the time. Didn't we Jerry? Just before the time you transferred to Castlebrough to get made up as a driver."

"Yes," Your Father-in-law was the signalman. If I remember right. George Clark. You married his daughter, didn't you Chalky?"

"Yes," Chalky replied. "That's why I remember it so well after, - what is it now? seventeen years. Yes, seventeen years last Valentine's Day. Some Valentine's day for my missus and family. George couldn't eat or sleep for years after. Never got into a cabin again, Ended up sweeping Paragon platforms. That crash finished him. Didn't live long."

Joe added knowingly. "Just like last year's crash at Castlebrough. The signalman there pulled the wrong signal. I was derailed at Heslerton by the signalwoman last year. Seems like signalmen are mostly at fault."

Chalky White and Jerry laughed, almost in unison. "Don't you believe it son. Loco men cause their share," replied Chalky. "Just a week before the Valentine's day crash there'd been a sidelong crash between two passenger trains going into Paragon. On the same spot just outside Park Street cabin and that was the driver's mistake. The pilotman's mistake really, the Halifax driver didn't know the way into Paragon and he had a pilotman telling him the signals. Trouble was that the pilotman misread the signals."

"That was a Halifax express and a Hornsea incoming passenger." Jerry added, "That was a lucky escape for the passengers, no one was killed."

Driver White returned to the crash for which his Father-in-law took the blame. "George Clark couldn't have made his mistake if one of his mates, one of the other two signalmen hadn't broken a rule."

"A rule?" queried Joe.

"You remember it don't you Jerry?"

"The one that says a signal must never be restored to danger until the whole of the train is past the signal," replied Jerry.

"Yes the Castlebrough train had his road laid and he'd got his signals which locked the points in front of him. He was travelling and part of his train was past the signal but his front end had not reached the locking bars when the signal was restored. That made it possible for two seconds for the facing points to be changed in front of him. That's what my wife's father did. He pulled 95 lever instead of 96 for the incoming Hornsea train. By that mistake occurring within that two-seconds period he'd turned the Castlebrough train into the incoming Hornsea passenger train."

Joe had been riveted by Chalky's account. His questions poured out. Both Jerry and Chalky White filled in the picture in great detail. Jerry had helped with the rescue and Chalky knew all the personal details about the family of the sixty-year old signalman. They told of twelve killed and the twenty-four injured; how the carriages on both trains had telescoped dramatically killing office workers and children. How the seaside resort of Hornsea had declared a day of mourning for its lost children and citizens. Very relevant to Joe was the instruction in railway working he was receiving from this dramatised account of the 1927 Valentine's day disaster at Hull. While he imbibed the experience, the time and the sandwiches slipped away and they had to depart Botanic loco shed.

On the short journey to the station he learnt as much about the route as he could. He thought, 'Maybe one day I'll be able to look out, shout a warning and avoid a tragedy like that.' He mused on as he prepared his boiler and fire for the return trip to Castlebrough. 'Although this tale might remind me not to eat the driver's snap ever again. I'll have to learn all the rules too.'

Their nine-coach train was waiting in platform nine. More passengers than usual grouped on the platform. They appeared animated. As the D49 loco bumped up to the train and Joe set off to couple his engine he realised the crowds were listening attentively to the station's public address system.

"What's the matter?" Joe enquired of the nearest group.

"The Second Front. Just announced that allied forces have landed on the north coast of France. Naval, army, and air forces. Biggest sea bourne invasion in history."

Joe rushed back to his engine cab and gabbled excitedly, "France has been invaded by us. It's just being announced over the public address system." He ran back down the platform to get away from the noise of his locomotive. Chalky White and Jerry followed, eager for the news. Amid the excitement Joe recalled that the racehorse's name was 'Second Front.' Surely there must be some connection. He'd make sure he'd back it well the next day. Everyone buzzed with excitement, but the train still had to leave when the hands of the clock had reached to 10.50.

* * * * * *

3
ANOTHER LESSON LEARNT

It was not long before all the men at Castlebrough shed learnt of Joe's habit of eating his mate's pack up. Some said they were going to place the matter on the agenda of the Local Departmental Committee; to be dealt with by the management and the men's representatives. Others advised Jerry to demand food coupons from Joe's ration book. It was suggested that drivers 'black' him and refuse to take him as their fireman. More irritatingly he couldn't leave his own pack unsupervised in the messroom, it would disappear, and only if luck was on his side would it mysteriously appear in time for him to eat during his shift.

The issue was further exacerbated by Joe's well meaning tip that the horse 'Second Front' in the three o'clock at Beverley was an almost dead cert. at very good odds. Advice he had obtained quite literally 'from the horse's mouth.' She ran well, coming in third, but everybody in the country had backed her and forced the starting price down to 'odds on'.

The funny side of the event soon started to lose its power to bring a smile to Joe's face. He was beginning to become a butt for the attention of senior cleaners on those days he had to spend in the shed on cleaning duties and the general lack of supervision led to all types of bullying practices. Joe was buried up to his neck in the warm sand of the shed sand pit with his hands tied behind his back and a sandwich left under his nose. After a period of taunting he was left alone and was later reported to Bill Clarke as, "said to be asleep in the sand pit while we are cleaning engines." Clarke had him dug out and seriously warned "Don't let it happen again. You'll be for the high jump next time?"

Joe tried facing up to the bullies individually, but each confrontation would be followed by another gang attack. He found that his best strategy was to suffer each attack with little show of hostility and rebellion, keep his head down and disappear as soon as some other, lowly, yelling individual was picked on by the gang.

Popular frolics included forcing some luckless newcomer into a warm firebox and securing the door so that he could not escape or shrinking a new cleaner's cap on the engine whistle and blowing it high into the air after he'd climbed along the boiler to rescue it before it was shrunk beyond all recognition. The attention that new cleaners' private parts got from hot oil and axle grease bordered on the cruel and the sadistic. Joe learnt quickly to disappear when a certain gang psychology emerged.

Fortunately the need to use engine cleaners as firemen took him away from the shed and from the bullying of older cleaners into the more adult and demanding world of the footplate. But bullying continued as a feature of shed life for many a day to come.

Some days later after the joyful news heard in Hull, Joe told Jim Simpson how instructive he had found the detail of the head-on crash at Hull on Saint Valentines Day 1927.

"What about a mutual improvement class next Sunday morning in the Tavern spare room with Arthur Wilko if we're not at work?" Jim Simpson suggested. "Arthur Wilko is a mine of information on big crashes. He's always looking for an audience."

Joe was keen. It would be an ad hoc meeting, not a properly organised class. It was difficult to find a time when men were free from duty because the present demands of war caused nearly all men to work a seven day week.

Engine cleaning was his duty for the day. He had broken away from his task to have a short chat with Jim Simpson about the 'Second Front', the racehorse and the crash memories.

"Bloody soddin heathens."

Joe heard the painful protest of junior cleaner Mousey who was suffering the unwelcome attentions of the George Black, the shed's most unpleasant bully. The disturbance caused Joe and Jim to go their separate ways.

"Tie his legs to the big ends. I'll tie his arms to the eccentrics."

Mousey was yelling, not with fear but with hatred and threats, he seemed to know no fear of the bullies who enjoyed his spirited noisy rebellion. Curses fell from his throat as his three cleaner work mates enjoyed the struggle to tie him securely in the engine motions of the B16 which they were supposedly cleaning.

Joe peered through the driving-wheel spokes at the four struggling figures. "He'll get killed if the engine moves accidentally." Joe shouted with concern.

"Piss off or we'll tie you alongside him," Black shouted. "Better still go and fetch some black oil for his goolies." Joe disappeared as discretion whispered in his ear. He ran to the engine end to see if it carried the 'Danger 'Not to be moved' board. He checked that there was also one on the engine controls also because the B16 was in steam. "Wadey! Have you got that oil?" yelled Black.

"You do Wade and I'll bloody thump you when I get out,"

screamed Mousey from the confines of the engine motions between the driving wheels.

"Good idea. You thump him Alfred. We'll organise it," laughed Black. "Oil, Wade. Where is it?"

"The store was locked. Clarkey's not in," lied Joe.

"This oily rag'll do. Open his flies," commanded Black to his laughing assistants.

"Dirty rotten sods," yelled Mousey as the dirty rag was wiped around with glee inside his trousers.

Joe cleaned away with paraffin rags at the leading driving wheel and attempted to distance himself from the bullying three-some who eventually released their captive only to goad him more when he was once on his feet.

"There he is Alf. Wade, who said he was going to poke you when you came out," insisted Black as the tubby Alf Mousey was pushed stumbling towards Joe by Black.

"What you goin' to do now Wade? Now I'm out. You fetched oil and said you'd bash me," demanded the obliging, rough Alf Mousey.

"Nothing Alf," stuttered Joe."I said nothing," as he was pushed by Black to collide with Mousey who was likewise propelled forward.

"You bloody told us to back that hot tip. Dead cert' you said. Alf lost money on that didn't you, Alf?" Black was stirring the pot as hard as he could. "He deserves a bashing for that Alf." Joe staggered under the impact of Alf's body who obligingly played the role his bullying mates imposed upon him.

"I lost money on that too." The voice was unexpected. Bill Clarke the chargeman had crept up on the band. "But then again," Clarke said, glaring at Joe." I remember picking up a pile on 'Whistle Stop' when you phoned that one through last year." He looked at Mousey. "What you doing Alf with your dirty flies open. Get fastened up and get on with some work." He turned back to Joe "Is it you Joe that's leading 'em all into skiveing?"

"It's him causing trouble Bill," grinned Black. "Stopping us from working."

"I'd better give him summat else to do. A couple of tickets to take out."

"Whose?" questioned Joe with a quiver of relief in his voice.

"Cammish and Baker."

"I'll use my bike. I'll get back before two." Two o' clock was significant to the cleaners. That was when their shift finished.

Bill Clarke handed over the two small buff coloured 'call out ' tickets. "Don't come back, carry on home when you've delivered them." Groans rose in protest from the others but Clarke hadn't finished yet. "Get this engine finished you lot. You Alf, get cleaned up and take some gear for me up to Mr Franker's office.

Alf Mousey and Joe were delighted to be relieved of the unpleasant job of cleaning the battered, grease begrimed B16. They left like friends with a feeling of triumph as a result of their escape but vowing one day would extract their revenge.

* *

Jim Simpson leaned on the lounge bar in the 'Railway Tavern'. His navy pin-striped suit and wide-brimmed blue trilby marked him out from the uniformed railwaymen and the two soldiers who formed the small company around him. "I'd put a week's wages on it," he was saying. "There'll be a Labour Government after the war."

Joe was with the group. As soon as the class finished at lunch-time he was due to relieve the men on a ballast train at Sander station, so he was attired for work. Rotund, jolly Arthur Wilko was present, Joe was pleased to see, but his joy was somewhat reduced by the sight of bully Black in the company.

"Hope it gives me my job back after the war," said one of the soldiers in response to Jim.

"What job's that?" asked Joe.

"On the footplate at the shed" the local soldier Fred Green replied, then added by way of explanation. "I was a passed cleaner here before you started but I left so I could join the army."

"You'll get your job back after the war," stated Joe emphatically.

"Will I Jim?" Fred addressed Jim Simpson who replied. "You know that this job is essential work and as such it was forbidden to leave it and join up."

"Yes but lots of blokes left so they could join up," acknowledged Fred.

"The unions will try to get your job back but they can't promise. The problem is that when you come back you'll push back lads like Joe who started after you left."

"Come on," cut in Arthur Wilko," let's go where it's a bit more private so's I can tell you about the Gretna crash that killed 226 people." He picked up his glass and made off to a small private room where they could sit and talk.

"What's the point of talking about crashes?" George Black

asked pointedly.

"There's a lot to learn from mistakes. In fact that's the way forward. If you know what's gone wrong in the past you can take action to stop it happening again," insisted Arthur as he halted.

"But 226 killed you said," returned George. "That isn't going to happen again. Were you there Arthur?"

"No, I was a passed cleaner at Newcastle. Just a few months after I'd started on the North Eastern Railway. Happened on my birthday May 22nd 1915. The Great War had been on about six months. The dead were nearly all troops."

"Just before I started," said Jim Simpson. "I well remember that crash. It involved five trains. And a fireman was charged with manslaughter."

"And two signalmen also," added Arthur.

"Yes. You tell it Arthur," said Jim.

"I will do if you've got drinks in. Yes, mine's a pint of mild Joe seeing you're going."

"I'll have a pint too, Joe seeing you're paying." George Black instructed Joe who ignored the order but supplied Driver Arthur Wilko with a gratuitous pint and then settled down to hear the tale and discussions unfold.

Arthur told how on a bright sunny morning at nearly seven o'clock a local train had been shunted over onto a facing line at by a signal cabin called Quintinshill just north of Gretna to let two express trains pass. Mistakes were made by a fireman and two signalmen that resulted in five trains crashing and catching fire as gas tanks used for carriage lighting exploded. Arthur's eloquent description of the burning horror that consumed more lives than any other railway disaster held his audience.

"The main lesson for a loco fireman was 'Always carry out Rule 55 and protect your train. Even if it looks so unnecessary." Arthur looked at Joe. "What would that have meant you should do Joe if your train is put over on a facing main line?" asked Arthur.

"I'd have gone to the signal cabin to sign the train book and remind the signalman that my train was blocking the facing main. Make sure he knew where my train was stood." Joe returned his answer with confidence.

"Is that all?" asked Arthur.

"I'd have asked if he'd got my train protected with a locking collar on the signal lever controlling the protecting signal," Joe paused, "and I'd have asked if he'd blocked back to the signal box where the train came from."

"Blocked back?" interposed the surprised George Black. "What's that?"

"Blocking back," Joe replied. "He'd have sent 'Train on Line signal' to the box in the rear and that would have stopped the other signalman from even offering another train."

George Black's face exhibited annoyance. He felt corrected and instructed by the junior Joe. He asked, "Didn't the fireman go to the box and sign the book, Arthur?"

"Yes he did, but he didn't ask to see the collar placed on the signal lever."

"Why? Did he forget?"

"He said that the train was right outside the box and could easily be seen by the two signalmen and anyone else in the box. There were about ten railwaymen in that box that morning discussing the war news. The signalman simply forgot that it was stood there, and when Gretna offered the express he accepted it and pulled all his signals off."

"He couldn't have done that if the locking collar had been in place, and that would have reminded him that the train was blocking his mainline," added Joe to the evident irritation of George Black.

"The express came at speed and ran into the back of the standing local passenger train. Then a troop train from the other direction with 500 troops on board ran into the wreckage. Two empty coal trains standing in the loop lines were caught up in the wreckage. Two hundred and twenty-six died. The biggest most costly railway accident ever to happen in Great Britain. The whole pile of wooden coaches caught fire as gas tanks burst and it burned for 24 hours. The fire consumed the living and the dead. The nation was horrified."

"Surely they didn't blame the fireman?" The listening group gasped and broke into animated discussion. Arthur Wilko and Jim Simpson filled out the details of the disaster and the lessons learned.

Yes, the fireman and the two signalmen where blamed and charged with killing named persons by causing the collision. The case against the fireman was dropped. The two signalmen were found guilty and given three years in prison. Yes, they had suffered terribly. Both had serious nervous breakdowns. They were released on mercy grounds after one year in prison. The discussion hung on whether the full and proper execution of Rule Fifty-five by the fireman would have avoided the collision. The answer agreed by all was 'yes'. The catalogue of mistakes and errors created by the signalmen's actions could not have taken place if Fireman Hutchinson had seen to it that the protective collar had been in place.

Joe silently resolved that he would pay great attention to Rule 55 in future. Even to the point of going beyond his expected duty and asking, "Have you blocked back and put 'train on line?'

Arthur commenced his instruction "There's been plenty of other examples of not carrying out Rule 55 and crashes happening. There was the Christmas Eve crash at Hawes junction on the Settle and Carlisle line in 1910 when twelve died. All because two light engines were standing at the advance signal and the signalman forgot about them. George, what should happen when a train or engine is stood at the advance signal waiting to go forward into the next section?" George wasn't paying attention and had to pause for a uncomfortable length of time.

Joe opened his mouth to beat George Black to answer and thus irritate him further but Arthur took over instead. "The firemen should have gone back to the cabin to remind the signalman that the two engines were still there. But they didn't. When the express came the signalman pulled all signals off and had two trains in one section. The express caught up with the two light engines and crashed into them."

"But it's not always necessary to have to go back and carry out Rule 55." Joe added proudly.

"You'd know then?" added Black scathingly.

"Not if the signal had been track circuited, I was going to say."

"Of course you are right Joe but then in 1910 that track wasn't track circuited. All signals aren't tracked even today. Always carry out Rule 55. And if you go to the cabin see if the collar is on the right lever."

"Don't worry. I will," concluded Joe as the class started to break up. He donned his jacket and pocketed his bottle of tea, he was delaying his departure until George Black had left on his way to the shed, he didn't fancy walking with him up Sander Road.

The rest of the day brought no outstanding events for Joe. He was glad to bring the ballast train from Sander, stable his engine and set about stabling an A8 locomotive left by another crew. George Black and Jingo Johnson were stabling a V2 loco in number 5 road and Joe had to place his A8 in front of the V2.

On the loco by himself with responsibility to drive it down the long shed yard into number 5 road presented Joe with an outstanding thrill, he was being trusted by his driver. He moved off, knowing that caution was of paramount importance. If he moved too fast and applied his brake harshly the engine would lock its wheels and slide out of control. Because he was to place his engine on top of the V2 that was in the control of Black and Jingo he had to take care. He halted safely, leaving a margin between the two locos.

He cleaned the fire and emptied the smokebox and went underneath to draw the ash out of the ashpan, slipping his body between the rails and the wheels to drop into the ashpit. As he did he was surprised to feel his peaked railway cap leave his head and to look out and see the grinning Black clutching it. Joe ignored the prank and with his long ashpan rake cleaned out the ashpan before climbing out between the wheels. Black was preparing to drive his V2 into the shed and looked out backwards to grin at Joe who gesticulated angrily pointing to his barehead. George Black pointed upwards to the boiler of the A8. Joe followed the pointed finger and witnessed his cap seated firmly on engine's hot steaming whistle.

He did the only thing he could, climb aboard his engine and blow the whistle to blast his cap into the air away from the damaging heat. He saw where it fell and scurried across to retrieve it. The leather cap band had shrunk dramatically; the cap would not fit his head. Anger flooded through him as he determined to exact a physical revenge. He left his engine and ran after the V2 into the shadowy interior of the shed.

George Black was now on the running footplate alongside the front end of the V2's boiler. He was pouring dried sand into the neck of the front sand box from a spouted sand bucket. Jingo was on the ground ready to lift a second bucket up to George Black. Just as Jingo took the empty bucket down and swung the heavy full bucket into the air for George to catch, Joe called out angrily, "You're not getting away with that Black. You're a bloody twat?"

There was no evidence that the message ever registered with George Black. As his reaching hand grabbed the upstanding handle of the full bucket his booted left foot slipped dramatically off the grease laden footplate. His vertical body toppled over after it and his left foot swung inwards beneath the overhanging footplate to become entangled in the valve gear beneath. His capped head swung downwards to strike the standing empty sand bucket and the stone block paved walkway. Blood flowed profusely from a gaping head wound. Jingo sought to hold the suspended figure. Joe rushed to help his feeling of vengeance gone.

"Hold his shoulders Jingo. I'll get his feet." After a struggle Joe added. "Let's take him into the messroom and lay him on a table." Joe felt as though he was in charge and the old soldier Jingo was doing as he was instructed. When the ambulance had taken blanketed, but now conscious, George Black off to the hospital, Joe finished his day's work. The roster sheet told him that he was due on for late shift cleaning duties on the following day but he noted with some satisfaction, Black wasn't cleaning with him ."

As he prepared to leave, the voice of Bill Clarke broke into his silence. "You'll have to come on the 5pm dusthole job with Jingo tomorrow Joe, in place of George Black, it's another firing shift for you." Joe nodded and felt some sort of twisted satisfaction.

On Thursday morning five days later he propped his cycle in the racks at Castlebrough General Hospital and marvelled at the fate that directed him to be off to visit the injured George Black in Ward 5.

"Now George," Joe addressed the pale-faced, bandaged head. "Are you feeling better?"

"Beginning to. Might go home tomorrow. They think I've got over concussion."

Joe handed over a little envelope containing two pounds. "Money from the shed sick fund for you. I'm the shed sick visitor and Alan Harker asked me to bring this up for you today seeing you won't get in for your pay packet on Friday."

"Thanks. And thanks," Black added with a hint of remorse, "for pulling me out of the motions the other night. You and Jingo. Tell him. He's on five pm dusthole this week."

"Yes I know. I'm with him. I'm firing in your place this week so it's an ill wind as blows no good for anyone as they says."

"Yes." After a pause he added, "Did you find your cap Joe?"

"Yes but it's ruined."

"Sorry about that Joe. I really should stop pratting about. Ask Bill Clarke to open my cupboard number 55 for you and you'll find a new seven- and-half cap in there with a brand new L.N.E.R. hat badge. Will you have it?"

"Sure. Locker 55 not Rule 55," Joe replied. He'd finally got his own back.

1
A MYSTERY PARCEL

Joe leaned his heavy Raleigh cycle against the low hedge of a house in Sander Close, his carefully hooded bicycle headlight threw a small circle of light on the footpath. The dense blackness of the cloud-shrouded sky made his search for number seventeen difficult, he detached his cycle headlight to aid his search and walked up the short garden path to examine the number on the house front door. 'Seventeen. That's it.' He knocked gingerly on the wooden door.

'Knocking up' at Castlebrough shed was Len Bostock's job, but this morning Joe had been called out at 5 a.m. to take over Len's remaining calls. Len had gone home with a flu-like illness half way through his night shift.

Joe's cautious knock earned no response from the darkened house, he used the metal knocker carefully so as not to arouse all the sleepers in the house and maybe in the neighbouring houses, he wanted only to call on George Roberts, a newcomer to the shed, whom he'd never met. George would know he was being called for the 5.45am station pilot. Joe's duty was to see to it that George was roused from his bed, he lifted the letter-box flap and peered in. His face was illuminated with an unexpected shaft as the electric light on the landing and stairway flooded into life. The key turned in the lock and a dog barked at the back of the house.

"You're bloody early," the well-built figure in shirt and braces grumbled sullenly at Joe.

"I've got to go on to Tom's yet," muttered Joe apologetically.

"Here take it before you wake up our lass," yawned the figure as he pushed a brown paper wrapped, neatly tied square parcel towards Joe. "Give it to Bill. Tell him I'll see him in the Tavern tonight about it."

"Bill?" queried Joe.

"Yes, tell him to bring my bike."

"Does he know where it is?"

"Course he does. Don't talk and wake up our lass. Don't want her to know." The householder quickly shut the door and Joe took the parcel and biked off to Tom West's where his knock on the back door earned the customary grunt and an "Okay."

The parcel rested in Joe's messroom locker. Bill Clarke didn't want it, and he didn't have a bike belonging to George Roberts. When Joe met George Roberts at the shed he didn't ask him what

he should do with the parcel, he didn't recognise him as the well-
built figure who had answered the knock that dreary morning. Joe
revisited 17 Sander Close, where Roberts lived, but the house
failed to resemble the house number 17 on which he'd knocked in
the blackout last Monday morning.

Discretion began to loom large in his considerations. He would
become the butt of shed humour if it became known he'd 'knocked
up' the wrong family, collected a secret parcel for delivery, and
then couldn't find the house on a later visit. He began to wonder
if he'd dreamt it, after all, he had been very tired when Len
Bostock had knocked him up and asked him to take over the
'knocking up duties'. But he couldn't have dreamt the experience
because the parcel in his locker was real enough.

The War was obviously moving towards a close, that was clear
from the reading of any newspapers, a view endorsed by the most
of the men at the shed. The Soviet Red Army was storming
towards Germany from the East, partisans were defeating the Nazi
forces in the occupied territories in Yugoslavia and Greece and
Italy was out of the war and almost totally in the hands of Allied
armies. Eisenhower and Montgomery with their forces had
liberated much of France since the launching of the second front
and were preparing to storm eastwards across the Rhine and into
the heart of Germany. Joe's dream of participating in the second
front assault as a steam locoman taking trains to the front line had
not materialised, neither had his attempts to join the armed
forces, these had been finally scuppered by his failure to pass his
call-up medical and the grade four result which he did not
advertise to his mates at the shed.

A few days after the parcel episode, Joe was at Nawton railway
station not far from Pickering. Joe's thoughts were not on the
course of the war, they were on the sensual young school girl
figures that were teeming across the surface of Nawton station
platform. This was the third day he and Bill Ankler had taken the
five coach train and its cargo of green and orange uniformed Lady
Lumley's Grammar School girls from Nawton to Pickering. As
the girls chattered and streamed along the platform to board the
train, many of their lively young faces, turned upwards, to look at
the locomotive and the faces of Bill and Joe.

"Joe," one of the giggling upturned faces addressed itself
towards the old tender locomotive and the grubby crew. "There's
a funny looking man in that guard's van," the pretty fourteen year
old laughingly shouted. She and the others in the past two days

had found enough time to talk to Joe and learn his name. Today they were in more of a rush than usual, the train was late in leaving Nawton for Pickering, the girls had to be in school by nine o' clock and that stopped them cluttering around Joe's engine for a few moments of the usual repartee.

"There's lots o' funny fellers on the railways," returned Bill Ankler from his driving position at the other side of the locomotive cab. Joe was reflecting subconsciously on the girl's clear complexion and recalling his own acne marked face. It triggered off critical thoughts of himself and his many shortcomings.

The week hadn't done much for his confidence, it had started with the 'knocking up' parcel fiasco and yesterday his written appeal to the Government for another medical examination had been turned down by letter with the curt words 'There is no provision for appeal against the medical decision of the Board.' Joe felt like a cross between a leper and an infirm inmate of Castlebrough's St Mary's workhouse hospital. Ankler's brief reply to the girl was punctuated by the sudden blast of escaping steam from the safety valves of Joe's dilapidated steam engine.

"God almighty! Can't you fire the bloody thing proper. Blasted me bloody ear drums out," mouthed Ankler into Joe's ear.

"Clear the wax out for you," shouted Joe with a grin as he took quick action to quieten his engine. He crooked a finger in the direction of the girl who told them of the 'funny man'. He indicated her to wait while he left the cab and made to join her.

"Where yuh going? We've got to get 'round this train. Get yerself underneath and loose off," Bill grumped into Joe's ear.

"Yeh, okay Bill. Just got to see this lass for a second." He knew that Bill had plans to depart from the engine while they were at Nawton and acquire some country produce for a prospective customer.

Bill reversed his engine and tightened the engine buffers up to the now empty five-coaches. He had brought the early morning workmen's train from Castlebrough to Nawton via Rillington and Pickering and the men had departed to work on the almost completed Osmotherby airfield. Joe and Bill had now to return to Pickering with the Nawton area girls who were due to attend the Pickering Lady Lumley's grammar school for their 9 a.m. lessons. Joe threaded his way through the green and orange clad figures, he kept a cautious eye on the tall sharp nosed Mrs Gray who taught at Lady Lumley's and who maintained a disciplinary eye on the girls as she and they journeyed each morning from Nawton to

Pickering.

"Yes Joe," grinned the cheruby, long-haired school girl cheekily up into Joe's acne marked face. "What do you want?"

"You said something about a funny fellow in the guard's van." Joe's question was not burning within him, it really did not assume any significance in his scale of urgent matters, but it did offer him the chance to go and talk briefly to some of the girls.

"There was a man in the front guard's van eating a raw turnip while he sat on a mailbag."

"How did you see him?"

"Me and Gladys looked in the van just now and saw him." She hesitated, "I've got to go Miss Gray is looking at me."

"Was he a railwayman?" Joe felt under pressure to depart because Bill Ankler was glowering in his direction.

"Couldn't be, didn't have uniform on. He was scruffy. Nearly as mucky as you," she giggled and grabbed hold of her impatient friend's arm and rushed off."

"Must have been one of the workmen late in getting off the train," Joe replied before hastening towards his engine's coupling. Ankler was gesticulating with a raised arm towards the wooden signal-post at the end of the platform with its drooping semaphore signal. Joe slipped his figure down the gap between the platform and the train and uncoupled the brake pipes and the screw coupling.

"Right away Bill. See you at the other end."

Their engine hurried away with Ankler's face displaying an obvious impatience. Joe knew the reason to be the delay he'd caused Ankler, who had a little unofficial business to accomplish at Nawton. He mounted the platform and turned in the direction of the other end of his train, Sam Fisher the guard, was walking towards him from the direction of the small station building.

Joe's engine was traversing the line of the neighbouring platform to move around the train, its trail of gushing exhaust steam fell from the chimney top and blew along the platform. The clash of its big ends, its rattling wheels and grinding brake blocks added an unnatural metallic cacophony to the tree-lined country station. The blue sky was wisped through with streaks of thin white cloud and a hazy Sun glowed just above the tree line. The drone of a small training aircraft reverberated monotonously in the distance but remained concealed from Joe's searching eye. The war was so distant as not to exist. Joe's mind wandered to the remark made by the girl about 'the funny man in the van'. No doubt she was having him on, trying a bit of kid. There were two vans on the five coach train, one at each end to allow the guard always to travel in the rear when the train travelled in an opposite direction.

Joe's curiosity drove him to reach for the handle of the van door, His eyes took a moment to become accustomed to the gloom in the almost window-less interior, they did not discern the figure which he was not really expecting in spite of the girl's certainty. A bag full of G.P.O. empty mailbags labelled Castlebrough and a bound bale of cotton waste for Castlebrough loco shed were all that occupied the van. There was the partly sliced turnip but no figure of a man, maybe there had been someone. His line of thought was rudely broken as Bill's engine arrived at the other end with a jolt. He ran off without having a word with the guard and quickly coupled his engine and made to join Bill on the footplate but Bill was missing, the engine brakes were firmly applied. 'God he must have been in a rush to go somewhere an' leave the engine without me on board,' thought Joe.

Bill was in the nearby platelayers' hut, a well-tarred construction of up-ended old railway sleepers with slightly sloping roof, out of which a cylindrical metal chimney spouted smoke and sparks. In the doorway the tall cloth-capped figure of ganger Jack Shipley leaned against the door jamb. Smoke curled from his ornate tobacco pipe.

"Jack," shouted Joe from his engine cab, "Have you seen Bill?"

"In here," Jack Shipley replied crooking his thumb over his shoulder in the direction of the darkened interior of the hut.

Curiosity got the better of Joe, he wanted to know what Bill Ankler was set on acquiring, if there were any 'goodies' he wanted to be in at the distribution. He was well briefed on Bill's ability to obtain scarce commodities from all kind of sources. The signals were in the 'on' position and a porter was placing empty milk cans in the front guard's van, girls were still boarding the train. Clearly there was to be no urgent departure to Pickering. Joe drew the conclusion that best suited his short term interests, he checked that the engine was secure and the boiler and fire safe to leave, and then set off to join Bill in the cabin.

The rectangular interior of the low roofed cabin was illuminated by two hanging oil lamps, roughly made seats covered with an assortment of old railway carriage cushions bounded part of the sides of the cabin. A glowing hot circular stove ate coal furiously while it boiled the inevitable cast iron kettle. Dominoes clacked on the rough wooden table that occupied much of the central area and tobacco smoke hung thickly burning sensitive nostrils. Breakfast was being eaten by the early morning Nawton permanent way gang of lengthmen. Hoes, spades, pinch bars, oil lamps and cans, scrapers and hammers were stored against the wall and in the rafters.

"What are you doing here?" Bill's irritable voice cracked out above the chatter and the clack of dominoes. Joe knew that the harsh question was addressed to him.

"Seeing I ain't missing nowt," was Joe's confident and to some extent insubordinate remark.

"We can't both be missing off the engine. Get yerself back and look after her."

"She's tied down Bill. Proper. Won't go anywhere."

"Get yersen back somebody might pinch her."

"Okay," replied Joe to punctuate the conversation and bring it to a conclusion but he made no attempt to turn to the door. Instead he quietly observed Bill's rummaging in a hessian potato sack. He monitored Bill's conversation with the heavily built platelayer whose main characteristics were a finger missing from each hand and a full drooping moustache on a sharp weather-worn face.

"Okay these'll do. What's yer mate want for 'em?"

"Seventeen and six pence - and they's a bargain at that."

"Got to take yer word for it, can't examine them in here wi' this lot looking on." Bill felt around in the sack and extracted a cock pheasant. "How long's it been kilt? It's quite cawd tha knows."

"Yesterday, about afternoon he were shot. He's fresher than you'd get in a shop if you could buy one. It's game tha knows. You don't eat 'em fresh anyway. Hang it in yer cellar Bill wi' yer wines and let it mature."

"Apples, tatis, carrits, two pund of cheese, a pund a butter, dried egg, bottle o' Burtons, a scraggy pheasant an' some other things." Bill paused, "At a guess, I've got to guess in here. There's about fifteen bob's worth."

"Seventeen an' a tanner my mate wants." responded the platelayer salesman.

"Well I'll call it sixteen bob." Bill never missed an opportunity to strike a hard bargain.

"Seventeen and a tanner. That's if tha' wants it. If tha dun't - ?"

"What yer pokin' yer neb in fer?" Bill snapped at Joe who was looking on and listening "Tha's supposed to be on the engine.

What yer doing here? Clear off!" He was aggressive, he pushed Joe away, he was annoyed to have Joe observing him having to shell out the full price. He shoved his money towards the platelayer. "Here better gi' it to you while I got it. I'm skint now. I'll have to sell some on it to get some of me money back before I get home and give this food to my old landlady."

The money changed hands while Joe diplomatically disappeared in the direction of his locomotive. The sound of signalling wire trundling along pulleys and the signal arm falling into 'off' position aroused his attention. The signal was the indication that his train was occupied by school girls and ready to leave for Pickering. He boarded the loco quickly, popped the engine whistle as a signal to Bill and the guard who was busily blowing his own mouth whistle and waving a green flag.

"Here! gimme a lift up with this bag." Ankler's voice sounded from the ground at the loco side.

"What yer got, Bill?"

"The less you know the better. Yuh should've been on here looking after things instead of poking your neb into my business."

"Better go Bill. The board's off and Sam's flagging us away."

The locomotive jumped forward as Bill urgently pushed open the steam regulator valve. As the train barked its way out of the platform past the small signal cabin and the platelayers' cabin Joe leaned over to Bill and questioned him. "Them fellers, Bill, coming out of the platelayers' cabin. Who are they?"

"They're working prisoners of war from Camp 83 at Norton. Jack Shipley teks 'em for work on the four-foot. Bugger's get paid for it too." The six figures all wore faded olive green peaked caps which Joe now associated with the armies of the Third Reich, they had been seated in the platelayers' cabin while Bill acquired his bag of 'goodies'. Joe and Bill waved in acknowledgement as they made their way noisily past the cabin on their way to Pickering, steam squeaked away from leaky piston valves and cylinder cocks and the engine exhaust shot high into the wispy blue sky. The few miles to Pickering station would soon be behind them.

The engine and train pulled into the almost deserted platform under the roof of Pickering railway station, squeaking noisily on the curved tracks, as it halted the uniformed school girls filled the platform. As soon as the engine was at rest Ankler squeezed out through the cab doorway to drop onto the platform.

"I'm going for a paper to the station book stall. Hang about. Don't mess around."

"Yuh want to see how the war's going, eh?" asked Joe."

"Bugger the war. I want the form tables."

Bill was only away for a few moments. When he returned, the station porter with shunting responsibilities was standing by the engine, a scraggy young man not more than a year older than Joe. He was just another sign that the war-time emergency had elevated young people to jobs of responsibility which in peace-time would not have been available to them until they were well into adulthood.

"Back her down to Mill Bank sidings when the road's made Sir."

"Don't sir me. You're not in school now," responded Bill."

"Just being respectful. 'Sir'," grinned the porter-shunter laying it on a bit. "Your goods train for Castlebrough won't be ready for half-an-hour. I'll get it put into Mill Bank for you then you can leave when it's ready."

With the five coaches placed in the sidings, the engine turned and the tank filled at the water crane, Joe took off with a sandwich in his hand. Bill was happily examining his acquired merchandise and pleased that Joe was 'off for a short walk.' Joe was on his way to see if anyone was on the train, had the figure in the van been a reality or had it left the train in Pickering station. He had kept an eye open in the station but hadn't seen anyone leave.

As he walked by his empty train he thought he saw the bowed head of a cloth capped figure in one of the compartments, he looked again more searchingly but if there had been an image it had gone.

He boarded the five-coach train in the siding by climbing up into the first guard's van, then made his way down the corridor examining every compartment for anything that had been left; papers, books, coins, maybe even a packet of cigarettes were possible finds. He'd almost forgotten the so-called 'funny man' when he stumbled on him seated quietly in a compartment corner.

"Hello," said Joe with slight surprise.

"Hello," replied the figure with an obvious guttural accent that marked him off as a foreigner, indeed as a German recorded Joe inwardly. The broad-shouldered man looked startled but not offensive, indeed he fidgeted and displayed a little concern.

"Are you going somewhere? I mean by train." Joe noticed the soiled flat cap on the head of the man of about forty, he noticed also that an olive green cap was folded and tucked in the pocket of the very worn greatcoat.

"To Castlebrough."

"This train won't be going to Castlebrough until 4 p.m. and then it's got to go to Nawton first to pick up the workmen to take back to Castlebrough. It'll be bulging at the seams too."

"Bulging at the seams? Seems funny to me. What is that?"

"Sorry," came back Joe. "The train will be full with workmen."

"Four p.m. you say. I've got to get to Castlebrough quickly. I can't wait that long."

"You can't travel on this train. I'll have to get the station master." Joe was standing in the open doorway of the compartment, the stranger moved in Joe's direction and grabbed his wrist with the possible intention of restraining him.

"No please! I be going to hospital." The guttural accent alerted Joe again.

Questions were burning in Joe's mind. With the forthrightness of youth he asked clearly. "Are you an escaped Prisoner of War? You're German aren't you? Sprechen Sie Deutsch?"

"Ja ich spreche Deutsch. Ich bin Deutsch soldat? Sprechen Sie Deutsch?"

"Yes," replied Joe in English as he realised he was getting in deep. "I only speak a very little German. I have some German prisoner of war friends from Silpho Camp. They travel in to Castlebrough to work and I'm learning a bit from them." He shook his wrist to break free of the German's grasp.

"Silpho Camp? You mean Silpho Moors Camp. That's where my son is. A prisoner. He was but now he is in Castlebrough Hospital after an accident."

"An accident! What?" asked Joe.

"He was timbering, felling, logging you call it. He's been crushed. I must see him. That's where I'm going now. That's why I want help."

"You are no good on this train. Have you got a travel warrant?" He continued before the stranger could answer, "Are you an escaped prisoner?"

"I am no good you say. No, I'm not escaping. I've just come from Jack Shipley's gang. Just learnt this morning after leaving the camp about the accident to my son who is a flyer. A clerk at Camp 83, a good friend of mine, he sent message, telephoned, to Nawton signalman. He tell me. Jack Shipley said, 'You thumb it Klaus to Castlebrough if you can be back on three o'clock empty workmen's train.' I ran off before he could change his mind. I promised not to 'clear off' he say."

Joe removed his locoman's cap and scratched his head. "How the hell are you going to travel without a warrant, a travel warrant a least? Have you got money?"

"Two florins. That is all? Jack said thumb lift on empty workmen's train to Castlebrough by mid-day. Walk to hospital. I do know the way. I've been on work party to Silpho. He said workmen's train comes back at three for workmen, empty. I could come back same way."

"Were you a Nazi?" asked Joe with a brutal innocent frankness.

"In National Socialist party you mean? In Germany you mean or in camp? It doesn't matter. I'm not National Socialist party. Never. I was metalworker, union branch leader. I voted against Hitler in 1933. I was in prison for strike, my members they go on strike and I am blamed. Two weeks in Berlin prison I got. My sons joined Hitler Youth and police let me go but told me to join army of Third Reich. I was captured by the Eighth Army at the last battle of Tobruk. I was with Rommel's Africa Corp. I've been in England since El Alamein. Two years."

"Klaus. You were a metalworker. What did you do?"

"Steam locomotive engineer. You call them, fitters. That's what I did at shed in Rostock."

"Your sons in Hitler Youth. Is that your son in hospital? Was he Hitler Youth? A flyer you said?"

"He was shot down over London. Never was good Youth Member?"

The privacy of their conversation was interrupted by the sound of goods wagons trundling slowly backwards into the siding alongside them.

"That's my train," said Joe. "To go back to Castlebrough. I'll have to go."

"I don't know what to do now that this train doesn't go to Castlebrough, Jack. Sorry. I call everyone Jack. I don't know your name. Can you please help me?"

"Call me Joe, the railway fireman. No friend of Hitler Youth or Hitler. Pleased to meet you? Hope your son will be alright."

"Well Joe, do you think I could travel to Castlebrough on your train?"

"That's a good idea. I never thought of that?" They both fell into silent thought for a minute. "But where would you travel. There's only the guard's van, our engine and the wagons."

The trundling movement of the wagons halted with the wrench of stretched couplings. "I'll have to go back to my mate. That's our train."

"Have you any idea how I can thumb a lift?"

"Not really but I'm thinking hard." He was thinking hard, he paused for quite a long time to show it. "You could stow away in one of the wagons. You'll have to get in a wagon or van. See if we can find one and you thumb your ride with us." The idea thrilled Joe, he was convincing himself that Klaus was not an escaping prisoner. Prisoners were a common sight in work gangs and often seen walking freely in pairs.

Joe led the way, he walked the corridors of the empty workmen's train to see the contents of the nearby wagons. There were some closed vans, empty steel hopper wagons for Thornton Dale stone quarries, two cattle trucks and a half-full open wagon of rough props or timber posts.

"You'll have to get in there. Can you climb in there?" Klaus nodded and followed Joe out of the nearest carriage door. In less than a minute he had scaled the wagon side and was out of sight among the props and posts. Joe made off to bring Bill and the engine to the train and await signal permission to go on the single line to Castlebrough through Thornton Dale, Snainton and Sawdon. His mind was in a busy state, he was trying to forward plan Klaus's journey to the hospital.

One little matter had been overlooked he realised as he coupled his locomotive to the twenty wagons. He didn't know the destination of the wagon in which Klaus had stowed away. He ran back to look at the wagon label. There were four similarly constructed grey painted L.N.E.R. wagons. He examined all of their labels until he found a consignment of rustic posts for Snainton. "Are you there Klaus?" he called. The answering call satisfied him and he made a mental note of the wagon number and the position of the wagon on the train. He thought of shouting to Klaus that the wagon would have to be shunted and left at Snainton and that he would have to vacate the wagon before then, the thought was left unsaid. Bill Ankler was whistling for the starting signal, Sam Fisher was walking back to his van when he told Bill, "The first stop is at Thornton. There's a good bit to do."

* * * * * *

2
A GIRL AT THE WINDOW

The way through Pickering was clear. At Mill Lane signal box they picked up the 'electric staff' single line working token that gave them permission to enter the single line as far as Thornton Dale. Joe leaned from the cab to take it from the signalman's grasp as they passed his cabin at moderate speed but the signalman cautioned them with a slowing hand signal indicating that he wanted them to stop.

"There's some cows on the line. Near Johnson's gates. Take care. platelayer's is out?" Joe repeated the message to Bill who'd heard it anyway.

The six cows were grazing on the long grass of the railway verge with the exception of one that obstinately occupied the space between the rails. Bill blew the engine whistle. Joe let the engine blow off steam, but the obstinate heifer refused to move. The loco crept closer but had to stop.

"They're out of that field, near that accommodation crossing," shouted Bill. "The gate's open. Get off and drive them back in." The instruction was for no other than Joe.

Joe scrambled down the engine side but despite his somewhat timid attempts the cows refused to take him seriously. Bill joined the operation, then Sam Fisher left his van to help. The cows played the game with pleasure. One attempted to squeeze between the wagons close by the one which contained the prisoner, it got its head beneath a buffer and could not back out to release itself. Sam Fisher had to carefully uncouple the wagon from the train while Bill gently drew the wagons apart to release the cow, but the cows still had to be cleared from the line.

Bill was feeling impatient. It wasn't part of his duty to leave his engine unattended and go and herd cows. He looked around to see if he could spot any workmen in the fields or woods, the platelayers were supposed to be out; he climbed up onto the fore part of his engine tender to get a clearer view of the line behind the van hoping there might be some platelayers back down the line. He stiffened as his eyes swept down the length of the train, he'd seen Klaus seated in the wagon containing props and posts. He left the cab with moderate energy and strode swiftly back to the wagon and the guard. "We've got a bloody stowaway aboard," he snapped out.

Sam and Joe turned from their efforts to marshal the cows. "A what? A stowaway!" exclaimed Sam. Joe was quiet.

"In this wagon." responded Bill smartly, punctuating his announcement with a rap on the wooden-wagon door. "Come on. Get out of there . . . ," he repeated, "Come on. Get out of there." The broad-set cloth-capped features of Klaus appeared above the wagon side then he climbed down. Joe was struck dumb, no ready response emerged. Bill broke the silence of tongues. "Who the hell are you when you're at home?".

"Whose he?" asked Sam Fisher of Joe when it became obvious that the stranger was looking at Joe with a pleading look.

"What can I do?" asked Klaus of Joe. Joe had to produce an answer.

"Can you help us get these cows in that field?" Joe pointed over the hedge.

"Yes, I used to be a farmer."

"I don't care what you used to be. What are you doing now?" asked Bill irritatingly.

"I'm going to help you with the cows, Herr driver."

"Herr driver," echoed Bill. He'd not been so addressed before and it diverted him from his purpose but Sam and Joe were moving to control the cows.

"Come on Klaus," said Joe.

He called him 'Klaus' Sam noted as they positioned themselves to herd the cows. Klaus was soon shouting directions to the others, he obviously had some idea how to control cows and, after a short while, they were soon cleared from the line.

"What about you then?" asked Bill Ankler in the direction of Klaus.

Joe answered for Klaus. "He's one of Jack Shipley's gang. Hitching a lift to Castlebrough hospital and back. Jack asked us to help." Joe was gabbling a bit. "I'm taking him to Scalby Road hospital, and then putting him on the green sentinel at three o'clock."

"The platelayers are here," said Sam as the two men joined them. "You're a bit late. We've done the job."

"Came when we could," answered one of the two strangers. "Hello Klaus. You alright."

"Everybody knows 'Klaus' except me," said Bill with bewilderment.

"He's a P.O.W. from Jack Shipley's gang. Jack got news that Klaus's son was injured in Castlebrough hospital and gave him permission to go to see him with our train."

"We should have put him in your van Sam. We couldn't get him in it at Pickering, there wasn't time," Joe informed his listeners. "So we lodged him in that wagon."

Obviously, Sam noted, the 'We' must refer to someone in authority. "Come on then. Let's be away. It's time we moved on." Klaus followed Sam to his van. Joe joined his engine at a run, Ankler was known to be wanting to get back to Castlebrough for the afternoon's racing so he took off rapidly without further question. Their next stop had to be the station that served the notably beautiful village of Thornton Le Dale and the nearby stone quarries.

The 18 mile line from Pickering to Castlebrough, known locally as 'The Forge Valley Line' was popular with Joe. He was familiar with all the signals, the road crossings, the gentle gradients of the slightly undulating line and all the yards, coal cells, docks and warehouses. He was only waiting for a driver to say, "Come on Joe. You know the road, you drive for a bit." He knew the secret of the single line working with the electric token and, he knew many of the people who worked the line and lived on the stations or nearby. Mrs 'Bony' Johnson, a retired station master's widow, very bony, long and thin, encouraged engine men to use her dry privy at the bottom of the garden, or to draw water from her cast iron pump in the yard, even to call in for hot water to 'mash' their tea.

At Snainton, young Carmel Burton would be waiting at her bedroom window in the crossing-keeper's house to wave to every passing train, her face aglow at each visit despite the death sentence she carried from progressive consumption. Everyone knew about her, everybody gave a statutory wave, engine whistle's blew in salutation, guards waved their green flags. Fewer people had visited her since she left her seat in the rose garden and retired to her bedroom, too weak to stand unless supported. Joe felt that he knew her and her family intimately.

He'd learnt from her mother how Carmel had been a brilliant pupil at Lady Lumley's, how good she was at art and writing, of her close interest in nature and the brook, how promising her career was until the dry cough beset her, how it gave way to hacking and blood in her sputum, to pains, weakening and breathlessness. Joe once told Station Master Tindall that he would like to meet her, he hoped an invitation would materialise out of his interest. His most recent expression of interest in her welfare had been the delivery of a two thousand word story written by him about a severely injured child, at fictitious Garthy Brook station, who had written a letter to a railway 'big chief' that had got her a special train ride and action that had changed her life. He had hoped his literary effort might amuse and inspire her. He had left his story for her only two days ago with the briefest of notes. He wondered how she might respond, indeed if she would.

They shunted Thornton Dale goods sidings, then on to Ebberston. They collected goods and wagons and delivered goods and wagons. They arrived at the passing-station of Snainton with no great effort and plenty of time before the next train to Pickering wanted to pass them on the single line.

While Bill was positioning coal hopper wagons over the coal cells and waiting for Sam Fisher and the porter signalman to plummet the wagon contents through the hoppers, Joe disappeared, on the pretext of going for a 'mashing of tea' he vanished in the direction of the train guards' van and Klaus and the detached railway house which was the home of Carmel.

"Are we far away from Castlebrough?" Klaus greeted him with the question as he arrived in Sam Fisher's brake van.

"About 12 miles. Only five stations away. Sawdon next, then Wyekam, Forge Valley station, Irton Waterworks and of course Sander Station. We'll be there, at Castlebrough before dinner, before twelve o' clock. What ward's your son in?"

"Cunningham. I think. That's how it sounded to me," he paused to search for words. "I have some - something to ask for. I must slash, go to toilet. What do I do in this van?"

"I don't know what Sam does in the van," Joe chuckled. "Come to think of it, I've never thought about it before. Has he a bucket somewhere?" Joe looked around the van. "You'll have to use the station toilet. I can get the key."

As they walked, they talked. Joe learnt that Klaus had two sons and that his wife aged 38 years had perished in the night bombing of Berlin. Franz was with the German army in Eastern Europe and Henrik was in serious condition in Castlebrough Hospital. Klaus had lost a teenage daughter with tuberculosis in nineteen, thirty-eight. When Klaus last knew of his own father it was to learn that he was in a prison camp before the war for communist activities. "They said he was a Bolshevik."

Joe raised an arm and waved in the direction of Carmel in the bedroom bay window. Her bed head was close up to the window and she reclined against a pile of feather pillows. She gave an answering wave, held Joe's letter aloft, then waved both arms.

"That's Carmel. She's sixteen but she's got consumption, you know tuberculosis like your own daughter."

"It's a killer," returned Klaus. "Pity Governments don't save persons... ... people, instead of having wars. Is Carmel going to die?"

"Yes, they say. They say it is now definite." Joe said with little emotion in his voice. "There's the closet, the toilet. I'll get the key from the Booking Office. Then I'll wait for you before I go to Carmel's house to ask her mother for boiling water for my tea can."

The black-painted rough back door to the railway crossing-keeper's house opened at his first knock. Joe saw the kettle simmering away on the fire in the black-leaded cast iron hob. Freshly baked hot bread cakes, buns and newly rolled pastry occupied the floured top of a scrubbed deal table. "Hello, Mrs Burton, Hope you do not mind me asking, begging I should say, for a mashing of hot water in this can?"

"Are you from the engine?" She asked as she took Joe's blue billy can.

"Yes, but this is my friend Klaus. He's from the guard's van. How is Carmel? She waved from the window as we passed."

"She's full on it. All excited, daft lass. She's more poorly though. Come in, both on yuh."

"Does her illness make her excited sometimes?" asked Joe as he entered.

"No. Daft ideas about things she'd like to do. She wants to be a writer. A poet. Come in, get yer can filled. These are me baking hands." She liked to talk, short, sharp sentences without waiting for replies. "You Klaus? Me sister married a Klaus. In America. He was a German American. Enough water Son?"

The friendly woman's torrent paused long enough for Joe. "Yes, your baking smells wonderful." He sniffed. "Bet Carmel will enjoy that."

"Bet you would, you mean. And Klaus."

"Sorry, I wasn't begging." He was embarrassed, he felt a blush creeping around his acne and over his coal-dust smeared face. He blundered on. "New bread gives me indigestion."

"Klaus'll eat yours. Have I met you before Klaus? Are you from Norton Camp working with the gangs?"

Klaus had to break in to the flow of chatter. "I've never been to Snainton. I'm from Camp 83 but I work with Jack Shipley's gang on the Nawton branch line."

"Klaus is going to hospital at Castlebrough to visit his son whose been hurt at work," diverted Joe.

"Carmel was in Castlebrough hospital. It's good, your lad'll be alright there."

Joe heard his engine whistle shrill and exhaust beats sound. He looked out of the kitchen door and saw Bill Ankler shunting in the down side yard. He was having to manage without his fireman. Joe turned back into the flagstone floored kitchen, recording how clean everything was in spite of the rough plastered walls and small windows.

"Here, I'm going to give you indigestion." She began wrapping four bread buns in grease proof paper and an old copy of the 'News of the World'. "Two for you too and two for the other two. One each."

'Thank you's' and, 'Your very kind Mrs Burton' flooded out of the grateful Joe and Klaus to the unexpected accompaniment of three 'rat-a- tats' on the floor above them.

"She wants some bread, or she wants to see you. Are you the fireman what's written to her, sent a story for her to read?"

Joe felt extremely embarrassed. He merely muttered "Yes."

"Cum on. We'll surprise her. Don't get too close. No kissin' like." she giggled. Her last remark seemed right out of the character image that Joe had created of her on the few occasions he'd met with her. They all traipsed up the carpeted stair treads towards the bedroom. "We're coming Carmel," called the firm round mother. Klaus followed them because the invitation had seemed to include him.

The door opened into a comfortable, substantial bedroom with large furniture, an old small wheelchair and a high single bed placed in the wide bay window. The iron fireplace was cold, the time of year made its use redundant. Catholic icons abounded, a wooden cross with the figure of Christ adorned the wall. A glazed picture of the Holy Mother and Child hung in the alcove above a little make shift altar with a lone flickering candle. Bibles, books and magazines lay around making the bedroom look a busy active place.

Klaus nodded his head in the direction of Carmel, then to her mother he quietly articulated, "May I?" with an indication that he wished to approach the altar. He crossed himself reverently, bowed his head and was seen to mutter an inaudible prayer then retreat slowly backwards. "May the Lord and the Mother of Christ be with you both." The mother stood silent and solemn while Klaus prayed, then she expressed her own devotion quietly. Joe hung back, uncertain and slightly embarrassed because he was unsure what to do.

They heard the rushed exhaust beats of Bill Ankler's rapidly moving locomotive. "He's just fly-shunting one into the small dock," Carmel explained and expressed some delight as she watched the loco and the shunter execute the unauthorised and dangerous fly-shunt. A speeding wagon was slipped by the moving engine into another road by quickly switching the facing points. "I've had a lot of rides on that old engine, a   J25 class" Carmel added.

"I really must be going when the sentinel from Pickering comes. We'll be following." Joe felt a little worried about his lengthening absence from his engine.

"No you won't, there's a forestry special coming immediately after that Dad says. You won't be away for another half hour. I know everything that goes on this line" she said quietly.

"You wave to every train don't you? Everybody on this line knows you are ill." He found himself concentrating on the dark hollows in Carmel's cheeks and beneath her eyes. She was still a pretty young girl, her hair still curled and shaped by her mother each day with the care that would have been taken if she'd been going to school. Her frailty was obvious, she expressed a physical tiredness but her eyes sparkled with interest.

"The trains bring people into my world. I think of it as my world of magic. All of you who pass by here each day are my world of magic. You come from the distance, wave or visit and then go off into the fields and trees. Today the trains have brought you and your new friend" Her speech was laboured. "You all bring me some experience of the world. Some ideas for the stories I make up." She looked more intently at Joe from her pillowed bed rest. "You must know I aim to be a writer when I get well. If you don't, why did you write me that moving story about Jeanette with her missing legs and, the hope that the railway line gave her?" The pauses in her slow speech were almost an invitation to Joe to answer her but he waited somewhat deferentially.

"After I got your story yesterday I prayed to Our Lady that you would come to see me one day. I didn't ask my mother or father to send you. I just prayed this morning as you went by with the workmen's train and as you waved I winged my wish to you and waved back. You see why I call you all my world of magic."

"I don't know why I wrote you that story," lied Joe. "But I want to be a writer too and I try to write."

"I want to be a writer, like Jane Austen. I write mostly poetry for the school magazine at the moment. I like Shelley and Wordsworth."

"My daughter wanted to be a writer," burst in Klaus but then appeared embarrassed. "I'm sorry."

"Did she become a writer?" asked Carmel.

"No." His embarrassment appeared more. "Entschuldingen Sie bitte. Sorry. I will not intrude my family into your life. I'm sorry."

"Please. You are part of my magic world also. You are from Germany aren't you? You came to see me with this fireman, with Joe. Please tell me of your daughter. Is she in Germany? Does she write?"

"The war came and ended our hopes. My daughter is dead. Margit she was called. My wife also. I did not mean to bring my troubles to you. Please forgive." Carmel stretched out her thin hand, Klaus's hand clasped Carmel's.

"You reminded me so much of my daughter, the same light hair and blue eyes. So like her grosmuter too, sorry, grand mother."

"You are sweet like my Uncle John," Carmel mouthed with a delicate charm.

"May I show you my daughter when she was young? And her Grandmother, my mother?"

Joe was a little taken aback by the touching exchange. He looked out at Bill moving their locomotive about the small goods yard, glad to see that all was well, the fly-shunt had not ended in grief as it could have done. Mrs Burton silently but approvingly listened to the developing tenderness between her daughter and the stranger called Klaus.

"This is my daughter, when she was sixteen, in nineteen thirty-six. And this little figure in nineteen-hundred was my mother. So alike they look." Klaus had withdrawn his thumbed sepia portraits from the bottom of a pocket sized tobacco tin. His hand held a small folded packet. "Do you see the alikeness with your daughter, Frau Burton?"

"Yes they are alike, quite remarkable" expressed Carmel's mother.

"Yes. I see what you mean Mother."

"You see why I had to offer a prayer to Our Lady when I came in. You reminded me so much of my daughter Margit. The sadness returned to my heart." He let his head shake slowly from side to side. "No, it is not sadness now. You have spoken and brought her spirit back to me. Whenever I am lonely I will think of you. She will always be with me when I think of you." The war-hardened emotions of the one-time Africa Corps German soldier threw a blanket over the tear that wanted to express itself. Carmel gripped his hand and shared a few moments with him.

Joe was wondering whether to seek to be excused. He was worrying about his absence from his locomotive but he knew it would be quite incorrect to bring Klaus into the bedroom and then go and leave him.

Klaus released his hand from Carmel's to carefully unfold the small flat package that had accompanied the photographs, seconds later a fine gold chain and small cross dangled from his hooked small finger. "In the photographs you will see this necklet. It is round my Mother's neck, and, it is round my daughter's neck. See the diamond at the middle where Christ was." The necklet passed from hand to hand accompanied by expressions of wonder. Carmel dangled it approvingly beneath her chin.

"Entschuldingen Sei," said Klaus as his concentration on language faltered. "Excuse me bitte. I forget myself. May I place it over your head. I would like to see you with my Margit's cross." He turned to Mrs Burton seeking approval. "You give me so much joy." He paused, expressions of delight and approval abounded. "Will you do me great joy? - - Will you let me leave it on your neck?" He turned also to Mrs Burton with questioning eyes.

"Oh! I couldn't, but I would love too. It is so precious to your family."

"My family are finished by the war. I have sons but no females. They have no females. I give it to you as my present from my family of memories. I would like you to have it and maybe when the war is finished I can come and see you one day."

"Yes, I will have your daughter's beautiful cross until you come and visit me in better times, won't we Mother? And I will light a little candle each day and think of your Margit. Mother will you bring me a candle and let me light it now?"

They talked, and expressed a warmth between each other that clashed with the hatred that Joe let flourish in his heart for Nazism and the German soldiers of the wartime newsreels. "There is a better world," he found himself saying as he listened to the voices which were so busy that his expression went unnoticed.

"I will write you a story Joe, a story about my little world of magic. I will send it to Castlebrough loco shed by the railway post," were Carmel's parting words as they left the bedroom. The rose gold cross graced her neck and the diamond caught a tiny magical quantity of light from the window and threw it into the room. Joe saw her as a vigorous healthy young girl with the best of life in front of her, she would get better and run through the fields and trees again, this devastating illness was just an interlude in her life's journey. There were no tears in her eyes because hope and faith occupied them so completely. Joe would be seeing her again soon, he promised, he would write in return by the railway post.

Joe and Klaus left with the can of tea and an even larger quantity of new bread and pastries. Joe's temples vibrated with emotion as they made their way towards engine number 1992 standing at the head of the small goods train in the platform. Bill and the guard Sam Fisher were on the footplate and showed immediate interest in the parcels and the tea. Criticisms were muted as Klaus and Joe joined them and shared their gifts. Bill added his newly acquired Burton's ale to his meal and his face seemed to express the pleasure of a perfect day and no sign of impatience as they waited for the forestry special to pass at 25 miles an hour and sound its steam whistle greeting for Carmel.

Joe and Bill were soon off down the pair of glinting rails into the trees and fields. Still in Carmel's world of magic, with whistles and flags winging their messages to the two diminutive figures in the bedroom window of the crossing-keeper's cottage, Joe was sure he saw the twinkle of the diamond on the cross beaming a message in return.

★ ★

"He's going to stop us at gasworks cabin," Bill shouted. "See what he wants son? He's coming to the cabin window." The signalman at Gasworks cabin had kept all his signals at danger until Bill's Pickering goods approached them. He lowered each one in turn as Bill crept forward finally bringing them almost to a halt alongside his cabin.

"Back into Gas Down. There's too much going on at Gallows," they heard the signalman shout.

"We've got to put the train in Gas Down sidings, Bill. We aren't going to Gallows Close. Damn nuisance, I'd written the route down for Klaus to the hospital from Gallows and now we aren't going there." Bill expressed no interest in Joe's problem, he obeyed his signals and followed the course and backed his train into the Gasworks Down sidings near Castlebrough loco shed.

Sam Fisher and Klaus dropped from their slowly moving van and with his shunting pole Sam disconnected the engine. "Off you go Bill."

Joe had a hurried consultation with Klaus. "Come to the shed with me and Bill. We're not going to Gallows Close yard." They mounted the footplate of 1992 and made their way quickly to the shed. Within a few minutes they had deposited their engine and were in the messroom looking at the morrow's work roster.

"What about an afternoon's fishing Joe, in the bay. Our kid's cobble's tied up and we can use it for a couple of hours." Johnny Marsay addressed Joe who was quietly accompanied in the messroom by his German Prisoner of War. Authority seemed to hang on Joe's shoulders. No one questioned the presence of Klaus although they recognised him from his clothes to be one of the working prisoners. Obviously, if it was okay for Bill Ankler and Joe Wade to be accompanied by a prisoner, it must be okay for them too.

"Can't Johnny. Klaus here has to go to hospital and I'll have to take him. He don't know the way and he's got to be back for the 'British Queen' at three o' clock."

"How yuh getting up there?"

"I've got my bike. But we'll have to walk. Can't get a bus."

"Borrow my bike," said Johnny. "Get it back to our house after the three o'clock train. Can you ride, Klaus?"

"Bitte? I not speak that good." The hasty colloquial dialect of Joe and Johnny had left Klaus wondering.

Joe took over patiently. "A bicycle. You know what that is Klaus?"

"Yes. I understand what is bicycle."

"Can you ride, work, make work, operate a bicycle."

"Yes, I can ride a bike."

"That is good." spoke Joe more slowly. "We'll go on bicycles."

"You are so good Joe. And friend. What is it of this world that makes us fight when we are friends?" Joe shrugged and Johnny started as if he was going to answer,but then thought better of it. There were a lot of men seated, or eating, or just passing through the messroom and a fierce debate could be started with the best of intentions. Joe made to open his locker and deposit his few tools and belongings.

"Bloody strange stink 'round here." Johnny's moustached lip curled.

"Must be you," laughed Joe.

"It's your bloody locker Joe. Smells like crap."

"No it isn't. Yes it is," contradicted Joe as the locker door opened. "There is a smell."

"There's a sound coming from that brown paper parcel."

"Bloody hell. So there is," agreed Joe. He was making an attempt to mute the discussion before all the men in the messroom were informed of the embarrassing sound and smell emanating from his locker. He plunged the small square parcel under his arm and his jacket and departed the messroom with Johnny and Klaus following. "I'm going to the bog to see what this is?"

The three of them congregated in the primitive three-seater water closet. Joe cut the string and removed the brown paper, he prised open the lipped lid of the tea-tin and revealed a stinking mass of rotting half-dead fish bait. A few bluebottles struggled out and made the three watching faces duck out of the line of flight. Joe's response was to let out a sickening note of revulsion and tip the contents of the tin into the water stream that ran beneath the three communal lavatory seats.

"There was a fishing competition on at the Mere last Monday. You must have been given the tin of live bait when you were 'knocking-up' and got to the wrong house." Johnny's analysis after he'd heard Joe's description of how the box had got into his locker seemed to fit the facts. Joe had called at the wrong house and the man at the door had assumed he was calling for the package even though it was very early in the day.

"Keep it to yersen Johnny. Don't want everybody going on about the stink in my locker."

"Cause I will. You know me. Quiet as a grave," laughed Johnny significantly.

"You'd better," replied Joe warningly. "Cause if you don't, I'll tell everybody about that highly embarrassing incident in the boss's office." Joe was learning fast how to survive. "You know? That one you didn't want anybody else to know about. . ."

* * * * * *

3
THE GERMAN EAGLE

"It's not visiting time you know," said the ward sister as Joe tapped on her open door and asked if they could see Henrik Gothen from Silpho Camp. "Who are you?" Klaus repeated the name Henrik Gothen more naturally and fluently than Joe. The nurse continued, "Are you family or friends?"

"Ich bin der Varter." Klaus was flustered, forgetting his language control.

"Family, father," helped out Joe.

"Did you have to come just now?" asked the sister officiously.

"Yes, we've come all the way from Nawton near Pickering and have to be back on the 3 o'clock train. Sorry if it's a bad time, but we were told that Henrik Gothen is here, he's seriously injured," replied Joe.

"Are you a guard?" she came back still with a hint of irritation. "Your not really dressed for it, or visiting a hospital. You are not even washed." A hint of humour, even teasing appeared in her voice.

"No I'm not. I'm off the engine. Klaus here was working on the railway with us at Nawton when he got news of his son's accident. I didn't have time to get washed, besides we don't have anywhere to wash at the engine shed. Not privileged like you here?" There was now a hint of insubordination and teasing in his manner.

"Well you'd better get yourself washed in our cleaner's store cupboard. Can't have you putting coal dust and germs about in my ward." Joe saw the Sister give a surreptitious wink in the direction of Klaus who had difficulty following the interchange of Yorkshire English. "Sorry Mr Gothen," she continued, "I'll tell you about Henrik. He's going to be alright. A large log fell on him from the lorry he was loading. He's got slight head injuries, broken ribs and a broken leg. He's going back to the camp sick bay tomorrow, beds are short here. You go and get washed son and I'll take Mr Gothen to see his son. Fourth bed on the left, in the main ward. We couldn't give him a bedroom to himself."

Klaus and his son Henrik were soon in deep and emotive conversation. It was now approaching the fall of 1944 and the father and son had never touched, or spoken together, or had vision of each other since Christmas 1941. Few letters had found a way through the tangle of war. Now they were both joyous and reserved, sad but very happy, both expressing a hope that the war was coming to a close and that the pain through which their family and others must go would be bearable. They communicated in low tones in their own language, trying not to pierce the blanket of silence that hung around the neighbouring patient's bed. Joe's approach triggered off a change from their native tongue.

"Henrik, this is my new found friend Joe who has been of great support and help to me. Joe, this is my elder son Henrik. At home before the war, he was great train follower, enthusiast, you would say, I think. As a boy he was going to become a driver of the big express trains. Maybe there is still time Henrik, when you get back home."

"Joe, do you mind me using the familiar Joe?" asked Henrik, "or should I speak more cordially of you as mister."

"You'd make me feel old if you called me mister. You are Henrik, I am Joe, and this is Klaus." His smile put the fresh-faced young German flyer at a measure of ease. The bandaged head and ribs and the plaster-covered leg constrained his movements and demeanour, he could not turn about to look down the ward, but he was relaxed.

"Your hospital is very good Joe. Your nursing people very friendly. They are so kind to a German flyer. It cannot be believed. Why, Joe is there war between peoples who are so friends?"

"I try to answer that to myself. But there is Hitler, Goebels, Ribbontrop. And of course Tojo and Mussolini. We should all get on a train together, let Henrik be the fireman, I would do the driving, Klaus would be the guard and the engine fitter. And we should take all those that want to live together on our train away from the warmongers. Let the leaders fight it out in a big field maybe while we clear off to Carmel's world of magic." Joe smiled at his own fanciful contribution to the conversation. "Has your father told you of Carmel? She cannot leave her bedroom because she is dying, yet she constructs her own world of magic that keeps her insulated and hopeful, even happy."

"Carmel," started Klaus. "She is so like our Margit that I thought I was with Margit. She was as if she was Margit back in life. I felt as if my family was coming back together. She was there and I was coming with Joe to meet you. Soon there will be Franz, the war over and our family nearly together. I took young Carmel to my heart because of her likeness to Margit. I presented her with your Mother's ancient cross, and promised I would come back after the war to see her."

The male patient in the next bed turned slightly in obvious pain. Nursing staff came to him and curtained off his bed.

"What is the matter with him?" with youthful ignorance Joe questioned a prim young nurse.

"He's a policeman whose been injured on the beach this morning. A sea mine had washed up and it was being dismantled when it went off. He's badly injured but should be alright, Some were killed, including a young boy."

'I wonder if he will get to know that he's in the next bed to a German airman?' thought Joe as he said, "I think I'd better go off and wait for you Klaus. We'll have to go for the train in half an hour. I'll be outside with the bikes."

The 'British Queen', a single car sentinel steam passenger coach awaited them at Castlebrough Station. Joe had bought the single ticket to Pickering for Klaus.

The presence of two uniformed auxiliary policemen at the ticket barrier brought home the nature of the risk. They were questioning the tickets and documents of rail users. Joe had no idea what they might be looking for but he decided not to take chances. He knew that he had been very lucky to come all the way from Nawton on the various adventures without anyone challenging Klaus's presence. Klaus could have been picked up by the authorities, he was technically a prisoner of war on the run and Joe was his accomplice.

"We won't go through there, Klaus."

"I don't mind them finding me. They will take me back to Camp 83," Klaus replied.

"But I do. You shouldn't be here. I shouldn't have brought you. Jack Shipley really shouldn't have let you go. We don't want to be questioned."

They moved out of line of sight behind a stone pillar. Joe removed his railway cap and exchanged it for Klaus's cloth cap. "You look more like a railway driver now," he said pulling Klaus's cap over his own head. "I'll show you another way in."

Joe was very familiar with Castlebrough station, having worked there as 'Lad Parcel's Porter Joe Wade'. He knew many ways in and out, but an exit door on the back wall of the station building offered him his best opportunity, he opened it from the outside by inserting two fingers under the wide space between the bottom of the door and the pavement and lifting the bolt that held the two doors. The couple passed through into the station and joined the green and cream liveried steam sentinel rail car on platform nine.

Klaus hung from the open carriage window. The guard blew his whistle. Looking deeply into Joe's eyes Klaus's expression was powerfully sincere. "I want you to have something to remember me with. It will mean more to you than it does to me. He opened his tobacco tin to reveal the German eagle badge that he had carried without any pride during his service with Rommel and the Africa Corp. "You have captured your German Eagle Joe during this tragic war." Klaus thrust the emblem into Joe's hand. "You have captured it with your kindness, not amidst the violence and fear of battle." He paused and hung his head. "Remember always Joe that all Germans are not nazi's. Some of us Germans have suffered more from the nazis than other victims of nazism. Think of me Joe as the German railway fitter who would rather repair your locomotive than fight you. Aufweiderzehn mien Freund. Du bist mien Kamerad" With a brief wave and "Dankeschon" he disappeared into the passenger compartment and the single-coach steam sentinel rail car took him slowly out of Joe's life.

1
MISSING PERSON

"Read this little notice Stanley. You know what we want. If I twist your arm you're getting it wrong." A bullying spree was underway in the messroom. Joe shouldered his way through the door having to push against the weight of bodies that struggled on the other side.

"Bloody pack up skylarking you three. You're interfering with our card game and snap," grumbled Frobisher the night foreman. His order was half-hearted but clearly expressed in the direction of the two passed cleaners who were struggling with a new recruit to the ranks of engine cleaners.

"Stanley needs a reading lesson Bill. Don't you Stanley? Say 'yes' when I twist your arm." Cooke, a large bellied 19 year old from the town's fishing fraternity was in the mood for some sport."Yes! Yes!" squealed the new recruit Stanley as Fisher Cooke shoved him face-up to the notice case.

"Bill, Stanley cannot read very well. Can you Stanley? You can't read them notices in that late notices case. You'll never make a locoman if you can't read. Will you Stanley?"

"No. Yes. Yes. I mean no," responded the small cleaner in confusion as his arms were twisted to the amusement of his two tormentors.

"Read that notice there. Go on. Show Bill how you can read."

Joe impatiently pushed close to Cooke and his bullying collaborator. He made to look at the late notices, he would have liked to have told Cooke and his mate to stop pratting about and leave the young kid alone but discretion was becoming a constant companion as he grew towards maturity. "Let me look?" he said as demandingly as he assumed was prudent. "Bloody Sunday leave cancelled again," he grumbled out loudly as he quickly and silently read the shed master's notice.

'To All Motive Power Department Staff at Castlebrough. Unfortunately, owing to the exigencies of the present emergency and traffic demands, all leave of absence has been cancelled for Sunday the 18th of December 1944.'
                    Signed F Franker
                    Shed Master.

"There's a short permanent way caution on at Bempton on the up line Jim," Joe called out to Jim Simpson who was to be his driver on the Hull goods train.

"Get out of Stanley's way. He's got to read them." Cooke blustered, aware that Joe's intervention was diversionary and obstructive. "Read that letter out aloud Stanley and I'll help you."

Stan had no choice. He responded in his usual manner when they subjected him to this special kind of torture. He knew what his tormentors wanted and he complied.

"Bloody Sunday leave cancelled again." yelled out Stanley taking his cue from Joe's remark. His tormentors guffawed.

"Do it properly," Fisher Cooke instructed. "I'll point the words out."

"To all - bugger it - sod it - Department men at Castlebrough. Sod it. It's getting hard, owing to the eggs and bacon and emery. You'll have to help me." They did. They pushed him on and encouraged his wider use off expletives. And when they felt they had sufficiently enjoyed his humiliation he was released but Joe was still there for Cooke's attention.

"There was a lass asking after you last night Wadey. Linda they called her. Knew you well. Said she fancied breaking you in. Firemen are a bit on the rough side she said. She really fancied you honest. Her and her mate said you reminded them of Clark Gable."

Joe knew that they were kidding him. "Oh yeh. She was outside 'The Number Eleven' I suppose."

"No, she wasn't on the game," answered Fisher Cooke emphatically. She was genuine. Used to go to Sander School with you. Linda Bakewell, said you were both in Miss Horseman's class. She was at the Olympia last night with Connie Brown. You know Connie Brown."

Joe knew Connie Brown. He found himself wondering who Linda Bakewell was. Cooke was renowned as a great story teller though, 'Bet he's fibbing,' thought Joe.

"Come on Joe we've got something different to do on Hull Goods today," said lean, active Jim Simpson, "and the snow's coming down faster."

Joe followed him out of the messroom and the conversation switched to politics and the progress of the war as they picked out their A8 locomotive in road eight. Joe hated cleaning out the cab of a filthy locomotive in the blackness of the shed in the early morning when soot hung thick in the air and on all parts of the cab. He was tired and unenthusiastic about his coming goods train journey to Bridlington where they were due to exchange trains and engines with Hull men who were working the Hull to

Castlebrough goods train.

The falling snow limited visibility. The five degrees of frost made the ground hard and froze the points, the sky was a dense arc without any celestial light. He had trudged to work in the early morning blackness with leaden feet, a railway uniform heavy greatcoat high up around his ears. Just out of bed he had donned his cold greasy clothes, refused to treat or punish himself with a wash, and left home without breakfast. The nearby houses seemed to snooze and advertise warmth and security. There was nothing joyous or enervating about his morning experience.

Jim Simpson pushed into the cab, the naked flame of his torch lamp joining Joe's in illuminating the cab. "You were saying Jim, that we had to do something different today."

"We've got to get a big load of tanker wagons through from Hull today. Castlebrough and Whitby are short of oil and petrol," replied Jim. "Don't really know what we've got to do, just that we are on our normal schedule of pickup goods to Bridlington, then changeover with Hull-Castlebrough goods and back,but somehow we've got to bring a load of tankers back."

"Have they given us a new train working, Jim?"

"No. Just the same working, but Frobisher said control had been on to say we'll have to expect some adjustments because they want the load of tankers through specially. There's a shortage of motive power at Brid shed. We might have to help somehow. Are you finished Joe?"

"Almost, are you oiled up and prepared Jim.?"

"Except for things here in the cab. Let's have a recap' Joe. You know how I've taught you to go through everything in order."

"Yes Jim, I can see me having a last minute check up just before they put me in me bloody box."

"Go on then. Have a check up now."

"Okay!" returned Joe. "The locker first. We've got 12 detonators, a red flag, spanners, two gauge glasses and washers, oilcan, coal hammer, gauge lamp, torch lamp, two headlights complete with shades and oil. Bucket, slaker pipe, only one firing shovel so we can't afford to break it or throw it in the fire. And this hand brush. All present and correct mate."

"You've a lot more to check yet."

"What?"

"Sandboxes. Are they full? Back and front. Is the tank full? Does the steam heater valve work? Is the steam lubricator filled up and switched on? Does the tap work on the tender? Have you tried the vacuum brakes, small ejector and large ejector?"

"That's your job Jim," returned Joe.

"They are all our jobs. If I overlook something you might spot it. Have you tried both injectors? Have you tightened the smoke box door?" Have you tried the sand valves?"

"How many out of ten, Jim?"

"Seven out of ten. But never mind you are getting better."

Back in the messroom they sipped their early morning tea as they listened to chatter of the men. A murder story was about to break into the news but it was already abroad on the grapevine receiving additional embroidery as it journeyed from mouth to mouth. "Murdered and cut up by a Polish soldier she'd met at the Olympia," proclaimed Stanley loudly, his face glowing at the attention he had earned from his remark. He certainly attracted the attention of Joe and Jim.

"What yuh rabbiting on at?" asked Jack Mild looking over his reading specs and his newspaper. The brutal description had interrupted his reading.

"She was killed and dumped in an inspection pit at Westways Garage." added Fisher Cooke as if he had definite knowledge.

"The truth is that the body of a young women was found in Westways Garage last evening," broke in Jack Mild the night-time steam raiser. "And the police are looking for a man of about 30 years. Nowt else's known. I live near Westways and the police were there in the street when I came to work. They told me that. I saw the body being removed. 'No marks on it' said the inspector to me. So don't go peddling crap you might have heard young man."

Fisher Cooke and Stanley dropped the subject and conversation erupted on the more important issue of 'all leave of absence for Sunday being cancelled once again. Some of the men welcomed the work and the extra money that the cancellation order brought them but it was now a weekly occurrence and it aroused anger in many.

Christmas 1944 was on the near horizon of time. Shortages, bad weather and the slow hard course of the war dulled the natural optimism of approaching Christmas. The final defeat of Hitler's Nazi Third Reich was within sight but still illusive. Von Rundstedt's surprise panzer counter attack in the Ardennes region of France had produced the 'Ardennes Bulge' as the breakthrough in American and British lines was known. Some alarm was abroad even though the setback was clearly only temporary. The bad weather of the continent, East and West, affected all activity and visited Britain with the same intensity.

Jim Simpson backed the A8 side tank out of Castlebrough Shed into the ice and snow covered locomotive shed yard. Other loco's were moving about so progress from the shed to the push bell cabin was slow. Shaded gas lamp standards threw some light around, three coal fired braziers burnt vigorously on their sites beneath the arms of the three water cranes, their duty to stop the water and the stout leather hoses from freezing solid. The A8 loco stopped near the first column; Jim and Joe had to take water on board, their small volume tanks had to be full to the brim to take them to the next water supply down the Hull line. The hard frozen vertically, hanging leather hose had to be bent by Joe in order to insert it into the tank, a hard task in any weather but very difficult in freezing conditions. Jim warmed his hands at the fire while Joe froze on the engine top. "We'll get a couple of tubs of coal to top up the bunker. She'll burn plenty of coal before she gets to Hull," Jim shouted up to Joe.

Joe obliged, after the water tanks had overflowed, he climbed down from the frozen tank top and held the rail points in position for the engine to back beneath the high level coal stage, then he climbed up on top of the cab roof to pack the coal into the bunker as it fell down the coal chute.

A gentle snowfall was adding to the snow-covered icy ground. The snow clouds hung low and threateningly, exhaust steam from working locos added to the poor visibility. Dark figures of platelayers, inadequately illuminated by hand held paraffin lamps, laboured on the tracks with shovel, scraper and salt, keeping points and signal apparatus free and working. In a couple of hours the darkness would lift, but snow and bad visibility were destined to accompany them on their journey with the pickup goods to Bridlington. Their task was to go as far as possible down the Castlebrough to Hull fifty mile line until they met and changed over with the Hull to Castlebrough pickup goods train. They made their way slowly in reverse past Washbeck and Falsgrave signal cabins and on through the tunnel to Gallows Close goods where their train and guard were waiting.

* * * * * *

2
SNOW BLOCKS THE LINE

Shunting small station sidings during the war years was an incredibly slow labour intensive task. Joe was always surprised by the passage of time and the amount of work to be performed at each country station. Each area or village served by a station relied greatly for its supplies of all goods from the railway. Coal cells, cattle docks, goods sidings and warehouses had to be shunted, cleared or replenished each working day. Joe's first journey on this very same pickup goods to Hull had seen him and Bob Laker relieved by a taxi-borne relief crew after spending seven hours covering the first seven miles to Filey.

Their task promised to be as difficult today as they left the Gallows Close with a string of assorted heavy goods wagons, still in the dark and with the snow falling with greater persistence. Five hours later and only seven miles into their journey they left Filey to face the bank and climb up to Hunmanby and Speeton. They hauled into Hunmanby station but the going was getting progressively harder. Some perishable traffic and livestock had to be delivered, but they could do little more work in the yards because slight drifting and falling snow had blocked some roads. The guard Tom Rittler and Jim decided to lighten their train by leaving some of the heavier wagons, which they assumed may be less urgently needed at their destinations.

With a bright fire, top boiler pressure, and sand being applied to the rails, they noisily faced the steeper part of the bank and the snow. They pledged that if Speeton signals did not stop them they wouldn't stop at all, instead they would take all their Speeton wagons through to Bridlington.

"Speeton's the worst place on the line for drifting. If we get through we'll get all of the way to Bridlington,"Jim advised Joe who was being kept busy by the heavy blast on the fire.

"Good that we've got a good engine," replied Joe as he stooped in the heat and glow of his fire box. "She should take us through if the snow isn't laid too heavy."

"Switch off the sands now Joe. She should keep her feet. If she doesn't, put 'em on straight away but try to save sand." The steam sand-valve was at Joe's side of the cab and easier for him to get at quickly. "Keep your steam pressure up and let your water level fall," Jim instructed. "You'll be able to fill her up as we coast down the bank to Bridlington."

"Thanks, but I'm alright with this engine. She's a good un. So long as I don't get a camel's hump in the middle," Joe replied.

The six coupled driving wheels of the A8 side tank locomotive had a good road holding capacity and climbed the rising gradient with relative ease despite the three inches of snow that had fallen on the rails since the passage of the previous train. A cutting breeze was carrying the falling snow across the twin tracks and piling it up in hedges and depressions, a sure sign said Jim that there would be drifting on the line to be faced on their homeward journey.

After climbing for ten minutes they were on the straight run up to Speeton Station; on a clear day they would have been able to see Speeton almost at the top of the bank, but the steady snowfall of large flakes obscured vision.

"Must be almost bad enough for the fogmen to be called out on duty," Jim called out. They were climbing to the highest point on the Yorkshire Wolds close to the coastline with the North Sea. Once at the top they would have an easy coasting run through Bempton and Flamborough down to Bridlington. They were on the lookout for Speeton's distance signal. Jim gave a long blast on his engine whistle; he was asking for his signals to be lowered and announcing his train's approaching arrival to Speeton station staff.

"Back board clear Jim," shouted Joe. He was sure he'd spotted the signal before his driver. "Does that mean you won't be stopping."

"If we stop at Speeton to shunt we'll never get up enough speed to break through the snowdrifts and we'll be stuck. Just past Speeton up to the top of the bank is a very bad place for drifting. You'll see in a few minutes." Jim was working the engine to its maximum capacity, the steam regulator valve was in full second port and Jim had his valve gear on thirty-five percent cut-off causing a heavy exhaust blast at the chimney head. Joe was working steadily with his shovel, careful to place every shovelful in its designated place in the fire box. He was pleased with his results; the fire displayed a brightness as an acknowledgement that it was combusting efficiently and the correct amount of discolourisation at the chimney top told Joe and Jim that all was well.

They clattered and blasted with their loose coupled unbraked goods train past the platforms, signal cabin and sidings of Speeton. The station master braved the snowy blast out on the platform to give them a cheery wave of encouragement; the signalman slid his window back and waved them on as hard as he could; they were both glad the pickup goods was not stopping to do shunting duties in the appalling weather. The train whistled back in acknowledgement and it was on its way into the mists of turbulently falling snow.

A sudden blunting of the train's speed caused a slowing of the forward motion momentarily and then the train resumed its earlier speed. They'd hit their first snow drift and broken through. The neighbouring line displayed the problem, rolling snow drifts from the line side hedge on the down line to Castlebrough were building rapidly; curling to form fascinating patterns at varying depths in the path of any train that came from the Bridlington direction.

"Put the steam sands on Joe," yelled Jim. "They'll help a bit." The train hit another drift, being almost dragged to a halt, and then it was through. Looking ahead on their line they saw their rails totally obscured by snow at different depths in assorted drift patterns. They weren't far from the summit but the drifts were thickening and becoming more numerous. If they were dragged to a halt they would never start again under their own steam.

They hit another drift, then another. The engine wheels spun wildly in spite of the sand on the rails. The driver had to close the regulator and open it again at just the right moment to help find her feet. "Not far now, with a bit of luck," yelled Jim. "If we get stuck, we'll close the line." His yelled message was hardly received by Joe before they hit the deepest drift so far. They struggled to keep going, the wheels spun, they had almost lost all momentum, snow sprayed outwards from the front of the engine as it cut through the drift only to fall back in front of the following train wheels.

"We've bloody well had it, Jim," said Joe believing he was speaking prophetically. Jim struggled with the spinning wheels and she found her feet and heaved on to gather a little more speed. She kept on and they were through another crisis to struggle on in the direction of the summit.

It was the last crisis. They were through. The they rolled slowly over the top in full expectations that the journey down the bank would be little impeded by snow. They were correct. The rails were masked with a covering of about four inches of evenly spread snow, but as far as they could see there was no obvious drifting. They drove more easily down the bank in the direction of Bempton through the biting wind.

Joe now had little to do but fill his boiler and keep watch, his shovel could rest. He was looking out of the left side opening over his driver's shoulder. Two rabbits skipped into the space between the almost invisible pair of rails in front of the oncoming train and paused with ears held alert. Joe urged them out of the way. They wouldn't make a dinner for anyone between the wheels and the rails. They heard him and skipped out of danger at the last minute to bound down the bank side in the flurries of snow. Their rapid movements down the bank disturbed something under the snow that was immediately clear to Jim and Joe as a boot resting, toe uppermost. One rabbit scuffed through the snow and a portion of red scarf flipped into view.

"What was that Jim? Something under the snow."

"Yes, it looked like it. Old clothes I think," Jim answered and gave a blow on his whistle. The signals were all at danger, they would soon be shunting Bempton Station. Jim was applying his engine brake and the train was slowing to a crawl.

"I'll just nip back there and see if there is anything of interest. You'll be alright without me for a minute won't you Jim."

"You just take care climbing down that bank," replied Jim. The snow nearly topped Joe's boots. The falling flakes soon lay on his clothing as he set off back up the hill through the biting wind alongside his train and passed Tom Rittler's van. Tom was leaving his van with his shunting pole in hand to shunt the yard.

"Hope there ain't much to do here. It looks like we'll have a job to get back home today," Tom said as he passed Joe.

"They'll have to get the snowplough out Tom if they are going to keep the down road open." Joe was looking for the tracks of the two rabbits in the snow between the rails. They were there, slowly being obscured by more falling snow, they were the markers that indicated the spot where he'd find the signs of the boot and red woollen scarf. They led him down the bank side to the bottom near the wooden fence that skirted the railway's land. The boot toe emerged from the blanket of snow near the dash of red down at the foot of the steep embankment. The difficulty for Joe was in descending the snow-covered, ice-hardened embankment, he alternately slid and climbed down until his reaching hand touched the polished toe of the shoe. His grasped assured him of the shoe's rigid nature; it was frozen, he pulled on it, and in lifting it clear of the snow revealed a trousered leg. He gasped, swept more snow aside, and moved the scarf. 'A body, a man! Good God!' More snow was swept aside. The fresh face of a clean shaven dark haired young man with closed eyes lolled over as Joe pulled on the clothing and swept more snow to one side. "Bloody hell! Who are you? Are you alright? Course you aren't." Joe was talking out loud. "You aren't stiff, aren't frozen. I'll get help." He pulled the limp figure up and dusted it free of snow. "I'll go. Here I'll cover you with my jacket. I'll fetch help. Hope you aren't dead."

The dash up the bank was conquered by Joe with an alacrity that surprised him. The run down the track to Bempton Station and his train through the muffling snow was difficult and exhausting. He passed the tail-end of his goods train and rushed down the platform to burst through the booking office door. "Where's the station master?" he gasped out with great difficulty. "There's a man on the line. Maybe dead. Unconscious." Breathlessness confused his delivery and response. "Got to tell my mate. He's shunting in the yard."

The booking clerk took over. "Harry," he called out through the back to the young lad porter. "Run down to the yard and tell the pickup goods driver and guard to come back up to their train. There's a dead man on the line. Well, maybe unconscious." He picked up a wall phone, cranked the handle and spoke into the mouthpiece to the signalman in Bempton box. "Jack, there's a body on the line between here and Speeton. Put the stops on. Have you seen the station gaffer?" He paused. "Good can you put him on. Yes. Tell him the pickup goods fireman is here. Breathless and distressed. He found the body. Yes, knows where it is. Good. You're coming over here, he'll wait."

The alarm had been raised. The message flashed down the lines. 'God' thought Joe. 'Hope the chap's still there.' Action unfolded quickly. The cold and snow made things more urgent. With the guards van and engine carrying extra passengers, the goods train was backed up the line in the wrong direction under Joe's guidance. The guard protected his train by placing a detonator on the line to warn an approaching train to halt. Six men including Joe, scrambled or fell down the embankment side to land close to the prostrate figure.

"Lord! He looks in a bad way. Let's get him up there into the guard's van," said the station master, who looked too portly and infirm to be down at the foot of the embankment offering to carry the man to the station.

"He might be - -," started the lad porter only to be loudly interrupted by the station master.

"He might be able to hear you. Be careful what you say. He'll be in shock at least. Let's get him somewhere else. Let's carry him

up and put him in the guard's van. This snow's going to be the
death of us, never mind him." Without a stretcher or any kind of
aid they manhandled the limp cold body up the embarkment side
and ultimately lifted the form into the guard's van that had no
comforts save a small cast-iron, coal combustion stove. Within
minutes the train was alongside the platform at Bempton station.

A hurried counsel took place on the platform while the
stranger, covered over with an assortment of coats and sacks to
warm him, lay close to the stove in the van. "Roads are closed to
Bridlington," said the station master, "So they can't get an
ambulance through. You can get through at the moment if you'll
take him in your van."

Tom Rittler rebelled at the thoughts of his van being an
ambulance or worse still being a hearse. "He looks bloody dead to
me, I don't fancy riding shotgun with a corpse."

"Someone will go with you. I'll go, and Harry here, the Lad
Porter. He'll come with you too." He didn't ask Harry whether he
agreed; he was ordering him to go.

"I don't want to go with anyone. I don't want that body in my
van."

"You're so sure he's dead. What if he isn't and you make him
stop here and he dies because we can't get him to hospital. How
will you feel then?"

"You take him."

"This train shouldn't go without its guard, you know that, Tom.
If I break the regulations and go with him in your van and leave
you I'll have to report that you wouldn't go. You wouldn't get the
sack but you'd be on the carpet, especially if he dies."

"You're givin' me bloody Hobson's choice. If I don't go to
Bridlington with the body in my van how am I going to meet the
up-coming Hull goods and get back to Castlebrough."

"Exactly," said the station master. "Come on driver. Let's be off
to Brid."

The man was made as comfortable as possible on a straw
packing palliasse and covered with carpets and blankets. Jim
Simpson and Joe boarded their engine, whistled for the signals and
waited for the unwilling Tom Rittler to wave his green flag and
they were off to Bridlington as quickly as possible. Flamborough
had received the word that there was a badly injured man on the
train so all signals were off as they rushed down hill through the
falling snow.

The ambulance met the goods train on Bridlington station

platform. Tom Rittler, disappeared until it had gone, Joe poked around the van, after all, he had found the injured man and he had some interest in the outcome. He was there when the stretcher emerged from the van but Tom Rittler was out of the way. The figure on the stretcher was totally covered by a full length sheet. Joe knew what that meant; they only covered the face for one reason. He felt sick. He collected his wet jacket from the Bempton station master without any enthusiasm; he thought of it now as a shroud. He was going to get rid of it. He mused, 'I lost my hat to Cooke and his whistle prank, I've lost my jacket to the undertaker. I'm going to have to take care of my trousers, somebody will have some designs on them.'

The pick up goods from Hull to Castlebrough was waiting for them to exchange trains. Jim took the opportunity to tell local control about the snow drifting on the line at Speeton Bank. "We are never going to get through without a snowplough. You might have to put single-line working into operation on the up line." When he saw the size of the train they had to take up the bank and the state of the train's D20 locomotive they had to use he went back to control. "You'll have to find someone to bank us or double head us. We stand no chance of getting even part of that load over the top."

The response was,"There ain't a chance. There isn't a spare loco at Brid. shed."

"What about double heading us with the station pilot?" asked Jim. "It's only a G7, on the small side but better than nothing." He persuaded his train guard, Tom Rittler to reduce the train load by removing traffic that could be left. There were twenty tankers that were badly needed at Castlebrough and Whitby, as well as fifteen perishable or essential goods, the load was still too big for the conditions.

They won their argument, the local shunting pilot was coupled in front of Jim Simpson's D20 tender locomotive. Both filled their tanks and sand boxes. Joe extracted some clinker from his engine fire box and raked forward from the depleted coal bunker the best coal he could find. He knew he was in for a struggle. Everything about the Dairycoates locomotive inspired gloom. Steam was wisping away from every conceivable joint. Lime deposits from leaking water joints were prominent, reminding Joe that Hull water had a lot of lime in it which, without chemical treatment, made it unsuitable for boilers. It might cause his engine to prime causing even more difficulties for him and Jim.

"We're putting single-line working into operation," said the station inspector to Jim alongside his loco while they were drawing water. "From here to Hunmanby. You'll have to take a pilot man aboard. The down line at Speeton is blocked now so you'll be working in the wrong direction on the up line."

Jim came in with a few questions. The inspector continued, "With luck you'll get up to the top and break through the snowdrifts at Speeton as you go down the other side of the bank. There'll be a passenger train at Hunmanby when you get there. He can't risk coming up hill to Speeton until you break through the drifts, - if you do."

"When's the next train through after us?" asked Jim, "From Brid for Castlebrough."

"It'll be here in ten minutes," replied the inspector. "He'll have to wait here till the passenger train at Hunmanby gets through to us then he'll follow you."

"If we're lucky. If the snow stops. If the wind stops. If this old crow steams and keeps her feet. There's a lot of 'ifs' in this situation." They were warming themselves at the coal brazier at the water column while Joe froze on the tender ensuring that the wide leather water hose stayed in the tank opening.

"What about the young man we brought from Bempton. Have you any news?" Jim Simpson asked the station inspector.

"Only that he's dead. He's been dead for three or four hours. He was obviously dead when you picked him up," came the reply.

"Who was he?"

"From Castlebrough. He had an identity card. The police say we haven't to say anything until he has been formally identified and next of kin informed," added the inspector.

"Tom Rittler is going to be pleased. He said he was dead and didn't want him in his van."

"The pilotman is coming out of the signal cabin. You'll be away soon." The inspector nodded in the direction of the flat capped figure with a 'pilotman' leather arm band around his upper arm.

The string of 35 wagons and tanks with two engines were waiting on the main platform for the journey up the bank. The signals were at danger. The level crossing gates were closed to the railway. Busses and bowed pedestrians made their way through the falling snow and over the crossing.

"What's your fire like Joe?" asked Jim of Joe who had just joined them.

"Not good. Heavily clinkered. Not very bright. The jets

blowing hard though so we'll soon have a full head of steam." Joe paused and inspected the gauge glasses, "The boiler's nearly as full as I dare make it. She looks to me as though the water's mucky and we might have to watch out for priming."

Jim seemed satisfied. As if he had quiet confidence in Joe's ability. He changed the subject. "The pilotman's coming from the signal box. He'll ride on the first engine 'cause that's in charge of the train. Do you know what he does, Joe?"

"I know that a train cannot go on the single line without him on board or a written ticket from him authorising it to go without him."

"More or less but - - ." Jim went on to instruct Joe in the secrets of working trains over single-line operations on double lines. The G7 loco in front with the pilotman aboard whistled for the signal and for the crossing gates to be placed in their favour. The cabin signalman waved his green flag and they were off, snorting and clanking the 35 loose coupled wagons into forward motion. A good start was essential, the slightest sign of slipping driving wheels was a signal to operate the sanding mechanism. They needed every ounce of steam to give them the best possible run up the bank which commenced immediately after the level crossing.

They were on their way travelling on the wrong line. It was a strange experience. They always ran on the left track of double main line tracks but today they were on the right hand track travelling in the facing direction. 'A situation which offers the chance of a head on collision,' mused Joe inwardly.

The snow was evenly laid, about eight or ten inches deep. A furrow, cut by their wheels on the way down to Bridlington earlier in the morning marked out each rail which carried about two inches of recent snowfall. It made progress more difficult but the two loco's hauled the train up the one in eighty gradient. They pounded their way up through the driving snow from which they had little protection in the unsheeted open cab of the D20 loco.

"She's not steaming well, Jim," shouted Joe. Jim acknowledged. Joe was not too concerned, he knew he was doing his best with a poor engine and coal in very difficult circumstances. He knew also that he had a good driver as his mate. He might well have had a driver that blamed him for everything that went wrong, and be constantly accusing him of making the situation worse. He'd been with such drivers, he knew of instances where fighting had broken out between the driver and the fireman in fraught situations where steam pressure was not maintained by the fireman.

"Come up here Joe. I'll have a feel at your fire with the fire iron. You keep hold of the regulator and keep your eyes skinned in front. If she slips her wheels, shut off and put the sands on. The driver in front will take the signals."

Joe was thrilled by the opportunity. He didn't think Jim Simpson was taking over the firing of the loco because he couldn't do it; Jim was just giving him a helping hand like Bob Laker had done on 2726 on the first mainline trip.

The boiler maintained steam pressure just so long as no additional water was added so the level fell inexorably as they pressed on up the ever steepening bank. Joe knew also that the water level shown in the glass boiler gauge columns was untrue. Because they were going uphill and the front end of the engine was higher than the back the water level in the glass was raised to a higher level giving a false reading.

"We are going to have to stop for a 'blow up'. We'll pick the lowest gradient just the other side of Bempton."

"Okay, what's the fire like, Jim?" asked Joe surrendering the driving position to Jim who had replaced the long hot fire iron on the tender top.

"Even, but not bright. Clinkered up. There's nowt much you can do about it except fire it correctly to get the best out of her. We'll definitely have to stop for a 'blow up' let's hope we can get started again."

"The donkey's stopped working again. I'll go out and bang the governor."

"Take care, it's blowing hard out there," warned Jim as Joe, with greatcoat on, left the cab of the moving loco to walk on the outside footplate along the boiler side and strike the donkey engine's governor with a heavy spanner. If he could not restart the donkey engine and keep the compressed air reservoir up to pressure the engine brake system would fail. He had to hang on to the hand rail in the biting wind and snow with his feet on the five-inch wide external footplate and strike the up-ended two cylinder donkey engine a smart blow on the governor. It responded, its monotonous but welcome beat sounding clearly alongside the heavier clear beats of the exhausting engine cylinders.

They struggled through Flamborough station and around the curve, both engines finding the going hard, they sounded their whistles often as they progressed up the facing line but Jim whistled the special call of , 'ta, rah, ta rah ta ta' then 'ta, rah, ta rah ta ta' again in order to attract the attention of the driver on the

G7 loco in front. When the attention was obtained, Jim Simpson
gesticulated in established sign language that they were nearly flat
out and would have to stop for a 'blow up'. Visibility was just
enough to enable the two to see each other. The message was seen
and understood. They managed to pass through Bempton station
and draw up onto a straight stretch of line with a less steep
gradient. Both engines were in need of a recovery period known
in Yorkshire railway parlance as 'a blow up' or 'a rally'.

"Check that the sands are working and shovel some snow off
the lines in front," Jim instructed.

Both firemen went out into the December wind and snow to
clear as much of the line as possible. They were not faced by deep
drifts, just a pair of rails out of sight under three or four inches of
soft woolly snow; enough to halt a train without sufficient
momentum, especially on an up hill section. The two firemen
worked as hard and as long as they could and cleared a long
stretch of the lines facing them. Their signal to return came when
their locomotives started to let off steam at their safety valves, a
glance backwards revealed the pilotman standing alongside the
locomotives waving them to come back. The guard had been asked
to screw down his van handbrake to hold the train while the
drivers rolled the engines and wagons backwards to produce slack
on every coupling.

"Wagons away," called out Jim as he put steam into his
cylinders and jostled to up to the engine in front. Together the two
engines started the front end of the train, skillfully pulling each
wagon, one at a time, into forward motion until they were about to
pull on the stationary and braked guards van. The guard knew
what was expected of him, just at the right moment he spun his
brake wheel free and the moving train yanked him into forward
motion. It was an operation that had to be done carefully because
the train could have broken in two if the guard's brake had not
been withdrawn at the correct moment.

The donkey engine was pumping away methodically, the
sanding pipes were pouring a thin stream of sand onto the two
cleared rails, both engines were exhausting heavily with their gear
levers on a very low cut off to give maximum start up effort. Joe
was peppering his small fire box with well placed shovels of coal.
They were off and they were hopeful. If the drifting was not too
heavy on the notorious cuttings at the top of the bank they might
break through. If they didn't they would block the line and spend
unspecified hours on the bleak top of the Yorkshire Wolds at

Speeton. The crews didn't talk. They worked and watched the dialled pressures and other readings.

They were past the place where they had rescued, if that was the right word, the man, his body, that morning. It produced in Joe a sadness as he looked out and witnessed the site. He had thought his vigilance had saved someone who would have died if he'd been left longer but the man had been dead when they'd picked him up. If the man was a Castlebrough man Joe hoped he was from a family not known to him because he didn't want to have to describe the finding of the body to any of his relatives. The train was now pulling up the uncleared rails and progress was harder, momentum was falling off, the embankment was being left behind and they were approaching the cutting at the top. Snow was thicker but not yet in impassable drifts. The steam pressure was just holding up, the water level falling fast but there should be enough to get them to the top.

"Did Tom say anything back there at Bempton when we were blowing up" Joe asked his mate.

"He was upset about having that man's body in his van. Said he knew he was dead when he saw him. Funny about Tom. He can't bear to see anybody dead, he says. He was a corporal in France in 1917 and he saw a lot of death. Can't stand it now. Suppose it's natural. He suffered from shell shock. Hell of a time he had. Did well to recover and get his job back on the railways."

"I understand how he feels," said Joe. "In a way I do. I left my jacket on the man when I found him. Thought it might keep him a bit warm. Now I can't bring myself to wear it. Somehow it has death on it."

"Burn it. You'll get another one from Franker. You have to tell him about finding the body. Ask him for a jacket then. Be careful what you say because you'll have to give evidence to someone, maybe at the inquest."

"I'm going to burn my jacket." He extracted it from the locker, emptied his pockets and tossed it into the engine fire box.

The train was hardly making any progress. The snow was laying thicker and signs of drifting were apparent. The adjacent line was covered in virgin-white sculptured drifts of varying depths. The train wheels were muffled with snow falling back onto the rails as it was pushed away. Both engines were on very low cut-off, causing a lot of effort and a lot of noise. Burning coals were spouting from the engines' chimneys and descending to litter the snow with black specks. Good fortune now graced the crews as the falling snow ceased and the sky cleared, better than at anytime that day.

"We're nearly on the top. But we're nearly stopped," said Jim. But somehow they just kept going. "The gradient board marking the top is somewhere in that snow drift," Jim indicated as the slope of the line changed slightly in their favour. They were moving so slowly that it would be possible to get off the engine, walk alongside in the snow, and then get on again. The cutting became pronounced. The weight of the train eased slightly in their favour as more and more wagons reached the top and felt the force of gravity start to pull them in the Castlebrough direction. Slowly the whole train passed the gradient board and started to help them down the hill but the snow lay thicker and still might well stop them.

"Look Jim! There's a group of platelayers digging out in front of us." The four platelayers were waving energetically to them to 'Come on.' The two engines responded to the encouragement. The weight of the train took them forward at increasing speed and, with their whistles blasting they charged through the snowdrifts where the platelayers had weakened them. They were through the worst. The snow had ceased and the bitter wind was less severe.

The engine boiler water level was so low that it could only be seen in the bottom of the glass with effort as the water shifted to the boiler front end. As long as the water injector kept working it wouldn't be long before the water level was more normal. They weren't worried, they were, jubilant. They had broken through and they had cleared the line for the passenger train standing at Hunmanby.

They drove into Hunmanby station with whistles blaring and crossed over to the up line on which they would be travel to Castlebrough without the pilotman. The waiting passengers saw the goods train's arrival as proof that they too would soon be on their way. The G7 loco uncoupled and with the pilotman joined the passenger train to take it over the single line to Bridlington. The pickup goods crew acknowledged the grateful waves of the passengers and set off to do a little shunting at each of the remaining stations to Castlebrough.

"You've given yourselves a job for tomorrow." Bill Clarke greeted them as they walked into the store at the shed after depositing their train at Gallows Close. "Fifteen of those tankers are wanted at Whitby so you two are rostered to get them through.
"

"That's good," said Joe. He liked firing to Jim Simpson and it would be interesting to see the coast road to Whitby in the bad weather. "Is it clear up there Bill?" he asked.

They've been getting through. Just like Brid line. Control thought that was blocked until you got through."

"That tonight's paper, Bill?" interrupted Joe, while picking up Bill's Castlebrough Evening news.

"Yes, you can read it," granted Bill after the event.

"Just interested in that story," returned Joe pointing to the headline, 'BODY FOUND AT LOCAL GARAGE.' They were talking about that in the messroom this morning. Mostly for Jim's benefit he read aloud from the paper. "At 10pm last night police were called to Westway's Garage and petrol station on Silas Street because lights were visible in violation of blackout regulations. The doors were found to be unlocked, and on entering, the body of a woman was found in a motor vehicle inspection pit. Police suspect foul play and are waiting to interview the owner of the garage who was last seen at 9.30pm.' Joe replaced the newspaper with an inward promise to complete the reading when the paper arrived at home.

"There's been a telephone call for you Joe, you'll have to tell your women not to ring the shed. You should know that private calls cannot be taken on L.N.E.R. telephones."

"What do you mean Bill?"

"Linda. She said you would know. She can't come tonight as promised. She'll see you tomorrow night."

"I don't know any bloody Linda's," exasperated Joe. Recalling to his own mind the statement by Fisher Cooke about Linda wanting to see him. Discretion warned him not to pursue the subject.

"Bill did you hear about us finding a dead man? Really it was Joe that found him and came back as white as driven snow. His face I mean."

"Yes, it came through on the blower. You alright now son?"

"Yes, been alright all the time."

"What time are we on tomorrow Bill?"

"Control have given you a road at nine, sign on at seven-thirty. You shouldn't be long taking fifteen tanks to Whitby unless the snow comes again," Bill informed them as they left the store.

Joe addressed Jim Simpson as they walked towards the messroom. "Do you think we should tell the police or Franker?"

"We'll go and see Franker now. You've already told the police at Bridlington. I'm expecting the police to come and see us for a formal statement. Don't tell anybody else, we don't want the papers picking it up from us. Let it lay. That's what I say."

"Let sleeping dogs lie. That's what they always say. I'll come and see Franker with you and then be off home.

* * * * * *

3
FOOTPLATE FISTICUFFS

The weather had improved, the snow and wind had ceased but crisp snow and ice still covered all surfaces. Walking home warmed him but heavy clothes were essential, he wore his cap, heavy boots and black serge railway issue greatcoat but he was cold, he missed the warmth of the jacket which he'd destroyed in the engine fire box. It would be a few days before the loco shed master re-issued him with a new one. The incident of finding the dead man had been reported briefly to Franker, he'd asked Joe to let him have a short written report overnight which should say that he'd found the body and soiled his jacket in the recovery and to request another jacket. Until his report was submitted and it became public knowledge via the press he shouldn't start talking about his find to too many people. To Joe that didn't mean he shouldn't tell his chairbound friend, Dan West. He called in to see him after tea and a change of clothes. Joe was telling his friend Dan of the day's events.

"Don't get more involved than you have to. They might fix you up with something. You didn't go through his pockets did you?" Seventeen year old Dan always expressed a suspicion of authority. He'd been that way when they were both at school together in Gladstone Road Senior Boy's School where authority flailed around with a swishing half-inch thick cane with a vigour that amazed and subdued the lads. 'Never volunteer for anything.' was one of his rules of living where authority reigned. Dan was involved in the craft of making coloured silver paper images on glass plates. They were edged with passerpertoo and turned into pictures which were sold to friends and through the shops. It earned him a contribution to the family budget.

"That letter to the Queen we were talking about. I think we should do it," said Joe. "Let's sit down and draft it now. Jim Simpson, the Labour Councillor said he'll get it typed for us."

"You sit down if you want. I'm already sat down." He spun his wheel chair around from the small craft table to face Joe. A bed occupied a large part of the council house front parlour. "I think there must be something doctors can do for me. Because there's a war on I was just put in the workhouse where they thought I would die and save them a job. Let's ask Queen Elizabeth to help me get into a hospital where they can operate and make me walk."

"That's it Dan, simple straight forward. A hospital bed where there's a specialist to look at you. Maybe you can get walking again and we can go into the navy together. A big hope, but you've got to have hope in this life."

The pencil traced out a draft as they pooled their ideas. No request for a wheelchair, no request for a job, no request for money. Just a place in hospital.

"If she can't pull a few strings Joe. I don't know who can."

It had been completed when Tom West entered the room clothed in railway cap and overalls. "There's a bobby to see you Joe. He's just been up to your house and your Ma has sent him down here. What you been doing son? Your Ma's going to be worried to death. You'd better go up and see her." Tom gave the impression that he would not stop talking until somebody interrupted him.

The policeman who'd entered the room interrupted him. "You know me. P.C. Johnson, the estate bobby. You're Joe Wade aren't you?" Joe just nodded. "I've been asked to come and get a statement from you about finding that body."

Tom West gasped, this was news to him. He thought the policeman was after Joe for some minor misdemeanour. "A body. Why didn't you tell me when you came in?"

"Never thought to."

"Hope you aren't going to be in any trouble."

"Nothing like that," said the uniformed constable. "I've just got to record the actual facts relating to how you came to find the body." His pencil scribbled away as Joe described his involvement in the finding and recovering of the body." He asked Joe, "Would you be willing to look at the body again to identify that it definitely is the same body you found?"

"If I have to Do you know who he was and how he came to be in the snow at Bempton?" asked Joe.

"Yes we know, he's called John Cooper. He was the owner of Westway's Garage. There's a report in tonight's paper about the body of a woman being found in Westway's garage. We've been looking for him."

Next day all the shed knew that Joe had discovered the body of John Cooper in the snow, Tom West saw to that. His listeners embroidered the news as it passed on.

Joe and Jim were allocated locomotive number 9885, an A8 similar to the one they'd had the previous day on the pickup goods to Hull. It was very suitable for working traffic on the road to Whitby, it would handle the 15 tanker wagons easily. There hadn't been a snowfall since previous mid-day and trains were working regular services to Whitby and Middlesbrough.

The line held no surprises for them. They went up and down through sharply undulating but constantly rising terrain of snow covered fields and woodlands to climb through the country stations of Scalby, Cloughton, Hayburn Wyke and Staintondale up to Ravenscar, six hundred feet above sea level. Many friends and acquaintances greeted them at the stations and gatehouses, if they stopped they exchanged conversations, if they didn't they merely whistled and waved. Joe felt the strong comradeship that existed amongst railwaymen, many times they shared more things than their occupation. The slow trip through country stations and the waved acknowledgements put him in mind of Carmel and Snainton, he hadn't seen her for three weeks but he'd sent her two short stories and brief notes. He'd received one note and a moving piece of poetry from her and they were developing into letter writers. He looked forward to another unscheduled meeting and hoped she was getting better.

"There's a Middlesbrough passenger train coming this way from Kettleness but I'm going to let you go forward to Robin Hoods Bay," the Ravenscar station signalman informed them. "You should pass him at Robin Hoods Bay. The snow's not been shifting so you'll have a good run down the bank."

Joe took the hooped electric tablet, which granted them permission to travel to Robin Hoods Bay. The words on the tablet read 'Ravenscar to Robin Hoods Bay.' While he had the tablet no other train could enter the section and collide with them on the single line. All he had to be sure was that he hadn't been given the tablet 'Ravenscar to Staintondale'.

"On your way, the signals off," instructed the signalman.

The day was quite bright now that the snow clouds had cleared. Joe and Jim appreciated the clarity of the day because they were about to coast freely down the most beautiful stretch of line and countryside on the Yorkshire coast and be treated to a wonderful expansive view of the North Sea from the amazing six hundred foot Ravenscar peak. With their fifteen tanker wagons they rolled into and then out of the short tunnel and down the snow covered, picturesque, falling rugged landscape down to Fyling Hall and then Robin Hoods Bay. Times like this Joe loved his job. With Jim Simpson as a mate he enjoyed it even more because they were inspired to discuss beauty and nature and extol the finer pleasures of communing closely with nature.

They whistled their way into Robin Hoods Bay station platforms. Joe took the tablet to the signal box and then they chatted while the Middlesbrough to Castlebrough train appeared on the horizon of the rising single line which would take them to Whitby.

"What's he stopped for?" asked Jim. The train had halted just after it had come into view. "Surely he can't be short of steam. He could free wheel in from where he is."

Joe was likewise puzzled. Five minutes passed, then the train puffed forwards slowly. "He's got going again. Maybe he's in trouble."

"If he is, he's coming. Go and see if they are alright. Might be mechanical failure or illness. I'll wait for you. If I can help give two blows on his whistle."

Joe was on the platform waiting where he expected the Middlesbrough locomotive to draw to a halt. The driver's face could scarcely be seen, his head protruded slightly from the cab as the train rolled down the country station platform. The usual stance for an engine crew when drawing into a platform with passengers waiting was for them to be looking out, side by side, acknowledging passengers' greetings. If Joe hadn't seen the driver's head on one occasion the train would have displayed the air of a ghost train, or at least a driver-less train. More suspiciously for Joe was the absence of the fireman leaning out of the enclosed tank engine cab offering to surrender his hooped tablet to the signalman or his representative.

The A6 locomotive, much like Joe's A8 locomotive, pulled to a halt, but no heads emerged from the cab. Joe grasped the hand rails and hauled himself up the cab side. The driver was seated with his back to the opening as Joe opened the cab door and entered, looking, in the first instance, for the electric tablet he required before he could travel on to Whitby.

"Bloody hell mate! What's happened?" The driver had his cap in hand and was mopping a profusely bleeding head with a clean but unhygienic sponge cloth, his dirty face was transfigured by riverlets of blood.

Joe grabbed hold of him as he appeared to sway. On the cab floor lay the fireman's hand brush displaying signs of blood. The Middlesbrough fireman was slumped with a bleeding battered face on the fireman's bench seat. He stirred and looked at Joe, who reached up and gave two pops on the engine whistle. Jim would know the meaning of that.

"Hi! Tablet mate?" came the query from the the porter out on the platform. He couldn't see in the cab. Joe obliged and handed the tablet over the side of the cab to the waiting figure.

"What the bloody hell's happened here?" asked Joe turning back.

"He attacked me with the brush," responded the dazed broad shouldered driver.

"You bloody thumped me you stupid git."

"Wind it down lads. Calm it for Christ's sake," broke in Joe desperately. "This'll be a sacking job if it gets out."

"It'll get out alright 'cos I haven't finished with that bastard yet. He's been at me all the way from bloody Middlesbrough about how I should fire his soddin' bloody engine. I'm not going another flamin' yard with him." Joe had to restrain the extremely dirty, well built fireman. He prayed for Jim's presence before the two started to fight again. As if he'd been listening, Jim climbed into the cab with a "What's up?" Then he saw. "Good God lads."

Another voice called from the platform, "Anything the matter?"

"It's the station master," said Jim after a glance outside.

The station master rattled the metal cab door. He pulled himself up to look in the cab.

"There's been an accident?" answered Jim.

"Good Lord. I'll get the first aid box. I'll call a doctor."

"No. No doctors," burst out the driver. The fireman echoed the message.

"You've got to get cleaned up and take the train to Castlebrough," Jim could see no alternative.

"And back to Middlesbrough," added the fireman. "Nearly four hours each way. With him? Not bloody likely. They can keep the flamin' job. I've had enough."

"Let's talk about the weather," tried Jim. "And calm it."

"Or sex," laughed Joe trying to lighten the proceedings.

Joe filled the engine bucket with warm water and both the injured men cleaned up a little before the station master came back with first aid equipment and very noticeably the tablet for their journey up the single line to Ravenscar. "Both of you look as if you've been in a crash and bumped your heads into the boiler," said the station master sympathetically.

"They did," added Joe to confirm it in the station master's mind.

"I ran into his bloody fists. That's what. He's bloody well been at me all the flamin' way from Middlesbrough because the engine won't steam."

"You touch me with that brush once more and I'll kill you, you bloody little bastard."

The station master became far more concerned. "You've got a full train of passengers to take to Castlebrough. You're thirty minutes late away now."

"You tek it then. I'm bloody up to here with it and the bloody railways," The fireman touched his eyebrows. "I'm not goin' another bloody yard with 'im."

"Bloody good job. I'm not taking you another bloody yard," savaged the driver fiercely.

"If you don't pull yourselves together I'll have to report to control that you wont go on and sombody'll have to come out from Whitby," broke in the anxious station master. "That'll mean the sack."

"Suits me," said the fireman. The situation was charged with emotion. "Let me help them clean up with this first-aid gear, before anybody takes any decisions." said Jim firmly to the station master. "Can you get them a cup of tea? You, Joe, look at the fire and the water. Get some steam into her. Come on you two. Out on the platform for a bit of winter air while I put a couple of plasters on."

Joe gasped when he saw the state of the fire; thick and burnt through but blue looking. The bars were heavily clinkered from the metal deposits in the coal. The air could not get through the firebars and the clinker to cause the fire to combust healthily. He sympathised with the fireman,who'd clearly struggled valiantly over the difficult fifty miles from Middlesbrough. 'If he can just get to Ravenscar top, he'll make it to Castlebrough because it's mostly down hill running from the top,' thought Joe.

Jim joined him in the cab."This is a mess. They'll not work together. The station master 'd be a fool to send them."

"They'll get the high jump if they stop the train here. Can't we help, Jim? I'll fire the train to Castlebrough if the driver would go with me."

"I'd have to take the fireman with me to Whitby. Do you know the working for these Middlesbrough men?" asked Jim emphatically. "They get time for snap at Castlebrough and then they come straight back with a fresh engine and passenger train to Middlesbrough. I don't think they're fit enough to do that."

"I'll go and come back and meet you at Whitby West Cliff if you think it'll work, Jim." Joe persisted. "Look at this fire. Could you get to the top of the bank with that? I don't think you could. You'd have to stop and blow up at least twice."

"Let's see if we can leave our train here and bank him to the top. I'll put the idea to them," said Jim leaving the engine to get the agreement of the Middlesbrough crew.

"We can't go on together," replied the Middlesbrough driver. His fireman nodded approval.

"That's it then" interjected the station master.

"No it isn't," Jim wouldn't agree. "These passengers have to get to Castlebrough. Joe will fire to the Middlesbrough driver and I'll take the fireman to Whitby West Cliff. We'll see how that works out. We all keep this little lot to ourselves for a while longer. There's one 'but'. This Middlesbrough engine will never get this train up that bank on his own without stopping for steam. We'll bank him up."

"Good I'm for it," jumped in Joe cheerfully.

Jim didn't ask for agreement, "Come on son," he said to the Middlesbrough fireman. "Get on my engine. You Joe get on their engine and I'll couple up to the back of the train and bank you to the top. I'll take the tablet at the back end."

Applause from the five coach train welcomed the two whistle blasts and the exhaust beats as the guard's mouth whistle and flag signalled the off. The passengers knew that there had been an accident on the engine footplate and were pleased that the crew had recovered.

Jim Simpson's engine did most of the work. The driver on the front Middlesbrough engine had been told to do very little work. "Just as much as you'd do if you were light engine. You've got to get some steam and water into her belly for the trip down the other side." The steepest part of the climb was a length of line that rose at one foot in every thirty-nine and through the short 'S' bend tunnel not far from the top. With a little help from the A6 engine Jim Simpson had no trouble. They reached the top in spite of the snow and ice and he saw his mate Joe away from Ravenscar for the down hill run to Castlebrough.

Jim put the tablet through the signalman's tablet machine and was authorised to travel back to Robin Hoods Bay. He collected his goods train and within thirty minutes had arrived at Whitby where the tankers were received by the Good's Foreman with relief. He took up a position in the goods yard at Whitby West Cliff Station to await the arrival of Joe and the Middlesbrough train.

"There is always a lot of falling out and tension on the footplate between two men." Jim was preparing to mollify his Middlesbrough fireman. "I know men who won't be rostered with certain mates. I know some that take the day off ill rather than go with some mates. You'll also know some?"

★ ★

Joe, on his way to and from Castlebrough with his wounded driver, did his best to placate the rage in the Middlesbrough driver's stomach. First names soon emerged and Joe was soon addressing his driver as John. They had a successful journey from Ravenscar downhill to Castlebrough but Joe lost no opportunity to explain how bad the coal was and how poorly the engine steamed. He broke the angry shell around his strange rough looking mate with his occasional informed chat and entertained him with the tale of finding the body, its significance to the possible murder, and his own expected visit to the inquest. The plans to write to the Queen for help for his friend Dan took driver's interest, he had a sickly handicapped daughter whose health care was suffering because of the problems caused by war. "The Queen might be able to help," said Joe. He described the sort of letter that the family might write about their daughter Lucy.

One event lightened the day for Joe, Carol Blanchard was one of the passengers on the train they had just pulled into Castlebrough station. She approached the engine with a smile of recognition.

"How nice to see you again Joe. More than a year ago since - -. Oh! but it's secret isn't it," she said mischievously rolling her eyes to one side towards her male companion.

The old embarrassments flooded through him, his ready banter faltered, his dirty acne marked face coloured in his perception. She was an attractive young woman, high heels, pretty hat with arousing red hair, and a coat that emphasised the slimness of her waist. Much different from the cheeky mischievous school girl who had inveigled an unofficial journey through Kettleness tunnel with him and Jim Woodley. Now, he wasn't so certain of his ground, especially when she had a male companion who had an athletic and academic look. He wanted to say, 'You never told your Dad the District Superintendent about your ride on our engine,' and have a light hearted flirt with her. Instead he mumbled on about seeing her working at York Station with the tea trolley and a few polite comments about the harshness of the weather. And finally "I'll have to go. There's always a guard or shunter blowing a whistle and waving a flag."

"Just one thing, Joe, I might be coming to live in Castlebrough. My Dad's retiring and is planning to come here and live. Might see you again. I'll get a pair of overalls and a cap for my next ride," she laughed.

"If you do come to Castlebrough. Look me up. I could tell you a lot about the railways in this area." His jubilant response was modified by exchanging looks with her 'athletic' male companion.

"Oh! Yes Jack, this is Joe I told you about at Whitby, remember how he had to go and bank a train though Sandsend and Kettleness tunnels." She smiled towards Joe and he flushed with pleasure. "We are going to catch the train to York now."

"We've got to go now," interrupted Joe's Middlesbrough driver. "Our relief crew are here," he acknowledged as Bob Laker and a Castlebrough fireman arrived to take their train and tell them that their engine and train for the return to Middlesbrough was awaiting them in platform 5. Carol and her companion, with slight acknowledgement, moved off and were lost in the moving crowd.

When Joe and the Middlesbrough passenger train drew into the busy Whitby West Cliff station Joe and John were like old friends. Jim Simpson greeted them on the platform and boarded the tank engine.

"Where's my fireman, Derek?" asked John.

"You aren't going to believe this but he's just getting a bar of American chocolate and two oranges. He was sweet-hearting an old lady on yon form and she said he looked tired. Would he take the chocolate and oranges for him and his mate. She is an old N.E. engineman's widow. Said she knew how rough the job could be some days."

"Where's he now?"

"Just putting her cases on board this train."

"I'll have to leave you John," said Joe, "Wonder where your Mate is?" Both Joe and Jim Simpson were edgey. They feared that the violence might break out again and involve them, at least in having to answer some difficult questions to the management.

"Oh he's here responded the driver nervously."

Derek squeezed into the cab, two oranges and a large bar of chocolate in his hands.

"I'm sorry John," he said simply.

"Me too," replied John quietly and just as simply.

"I was a bloody fool letting the engine get me down."

"Don't worry about it. I was too. Should've had more sense."

"That old lady I've been helping, she gave me these. Here you are John, half a bar of chocolate and an orange. Do you fancy taking them home to Lucy?"

"I do, Thanks, I'll take them home for Lucy." He took the offerings and grasped Derek's free hand warmly for a few seconds.

"A piece of chocolate for each of us and half-a-bar for Lucy," said Derek breaking his half-bar into four. I want to thank you two for helping us out." He grasped Joe's hand.

The driver added, "Without you two we'd both be lookin' for a job." Warm handshakes ensued.

"Is she a good steamer Joe?"

"Bloody good. Better than that one we had down."

"Hell. There's the whistle. That was quick. We'd better scarper. Before we end up going with you." Jim and Joe left the cab and from the platform looked up. "By the way none of that running will be shown on our train report," added Jim.

A hand reached out of the cab window and shook Jim's hand, "Thanks mate."

Derek's hand reached out to Joe, "Same here, pal, see you around".

★ ★

"This is a straight forward judgment," summed up the Coroner at the inquest on John Cooper. "A tragic case, but a clear one. John Cooper and Mrs Cooper were having a domestic quarrel which took them into the workshops of Westways Garage on Wednesday evening. They were joint owners of Westways. Mr Cooper who, as the evidence as shown, was ill with a serious depressive illness and was very excitable. The dispute between them was completely without foundation and was all in Mr Cooper's mind. It led to Mrs Cooper, being pushed, or caused to fall against the raised car lift, where she struck her head sufficiently hard to cause a head wound and an embolism which resulted in her death.

We know that Mr Cooper, left the garage in panic and was not seen again until he was found almost dead, or dead on the railway embankment. We don't know where he spent the night. But we do know, that he took the morning 7.25am train to Hull. The rail ticket found on him proves that. While on the train he wrote a note saying that he had caused his wife's death while in a stupid jealous rage by pushing her violently. He ran away in panic fearing she was dead. His note records his intention to leap from the train at speed and hope to kill himself. His body lay concealed in thick snow near Bempton until, quite fortuitously, it was spotted by two vigilant locomotive men. He might have lain concealed for days and the police would not have uncovered the facts of the case until he had been found. You have heard from the pathologist that Mr Cooper might well have been alive when the railmen recovered his body and took it by unorthodox means to Bridlington hospital. They might well have saved his life but chance did not fall that way. I find that Mrs Julie Cooper died from injuries received from misadventure, and that her husband Johnathon Cooper took his own life while the balance of his mind was disturbed by a depressive illness."

Joe walked away from the inquest in the police station. He felt a bit of a small star in the occasion. His name had been in the papers and his fame had earned him a persistent, female companion who had attended the inquest hearing to display herself on his arm. Her well enhanced bright red lips and bottle blonde hair would not have been Joe's choices, but then she had thrown herself at him, and she was good looking, The fact that her name was Linda Bakewell proved that sometimes Fisher Cooke did tell the truth.

1
PARTY PRANKS

"I'm going to the 'Tavern' for a few drinks before I go. I talk more easily when I'm tanked up." Whenever Joe was going to a dance or to meet female company, he liked to be lubricated with the 'juice of the grape', as he was fond of describing alcohol. He'd picked up that description from a reading of Omar Khayyam's 'Rubaiyat,' another of the educational influences to which he'd been introduced by Councillor Jim Simpson.

"There won't be much dancing at this shindig," Frank Sutton replied as they drifted up Sander Road towards Falsgrave Unitarian Church Hall for a New Year's get together. "There'll be some jungle juice at the Church Hall, bottled stuff."

"Yes, but let's have a pint in the Railway Tavern. And then let's have two pints in the Ship Inn. I'll be in good shape for dancing then."

"And talking rubbish. Linda Bakewell's going to be there. She's not giving up until she get's your trousers down Joe."

"I wouldn't let her tek our kid's trousers down. Never mind mine."

"I would," said Frank, "She's a bit of alright. Looks good, and hot they say."

"You never did have very good tastes," laughed Joe. "What they going to dance to - at this shindig."

"Music."

"Course, I know that Frank. Glen Miller's big band? A piano? Or gramophone records?"

"Don't know. All I know is there's going to be drink, a few eats and dancing, and of course," he paused, and with hand on hip danced a few steps on the pavement, "Girls, girls, girls, and more girls." The ice caused him to slip, Joe caught him. Their laughter and anticipation was not dampened by the hazards of the ice or the blackout; noise from other would- be revellers and the meagre road traffic accompanied them. The gauntness of the leafless December trees poked upwards as thin shadows against an almost lightless sky.

Celebrating New Year's Eve collectively in this way in a Church Hall was a new venture for the men at the shed. The little organising committee had broadened the invitation to other railway grades and even outsiders. A few station staff and goods station staff were expected as were platelayers and others. The approaching climax to the war promised to appear some time during the new year of 1945, and already a new spirit was abroad. The public were thinking of holidays, social life, and different clothes. All were thinking of the time when family members would arrive home from the war and things would start to change as dramatically as they did at the outbreak of war in 1939. The home-coming of Bob Cass from an Italian prisoner of war camp in Northern Italy was to be part of the New Year's celebration. Bob had been a fireman at Castlebrough at the outbreak of hostilities but as he had been in the 5th Battalion Green Howards Territorials he had to go into the services immediately. Now back home he was looking to take up his rightful place in the hierarchy of cleaners, firemen and drivers according to his seniority date.

"Thought you were late shift tonight Joe," greeted Johnny Marsay at the church hall entrance. A selection of dance records were whining around on a wind-up gramophone, the current waltz had coaxed a number of couples onto the pine-boarded floor. Simple christmas decorations added colour to the poster-decorated hall and the cloud of cigarette and pipe smoke. Posters naming the next 'Good Clothing Exchange' and 'Blood Donor Session' indicated the social nature of the hall. The food table attracted early, anticipatory looks and comments. Wardrobes and drawers had divulged more pleasing colourful clothes than the war taught one to expect, but that did not deter some who where attired in the uniforms of the L.N.E.R.

"Got called out early. I thought I'd have a night out," replied Joe to Johnny. "See what's going on here. Looks blooming exciting. Someone said some women would be here."

"They are. There's Jingo's wife, and them two unmarried ladies from the goods yard office, Mr Franker's bringing his Missus. He's coming, I think, because Bob Cass M.M. is coming. Franker 'll say a few words. Irene the big carriage cleaner is coming," laughed Johnny Marsay. And there's that little crowd of girls occupied by some of your worst enemies."

"Looks like being a real exciting evening," responded Joe then asked, "Bob Cass M.M. What's that mean?"

"Military Medal. Bob won a Military Medal for bravery under fire at Tobruk. Sergeant in command of a three inch mortar platoon he was. Kept his mortar position intact and firing under very risky circumstances near Tobruk. Captured by the Jerries, he was, met Rommel they say, spent the rest of the war in an 'Eye Tie' prisoner of war camp. He was awarded the M.M. in his absence, and has just received it now."

"Who's is the bottles of beer?"

"They've been bought with the kitty that's been raised. If you want one you've got to put into the kitty the price of what you drink. There's no licence here so we have to buy booze and bring it in."

"Come on. I'll get you something," replied Joe.

"Keep your eyes skinned for Fisher Cooke. He's up to something, been after you for a long time. Looking to take you for a ride but I don't know what."

The mild festivities continued for while. Mr. Franker and his wife came in with Bob. Hand-shaking for Bob and his old work mates, whom he hadn't seen for five years, was the centre of attention. The music had stopped and noisy drinkers around the bottle table had deferred to the occasion. The Shed Master said a few words about the end of the emergency being in sight during 1945, and a few more words about other lads who will be coming back to the shed, and for that matter, the goods station and the passenger station. "Bob is with us tonight after five years. Welcome Bob. Congratulations on receiving your medal" Someone played the record for 'For He's a Jolly Good Fellow,' and others made a brave attempt to get through the words.

Linda suddenly appeared on Joe's elbow. "Hello," he startled at the touch. "How did you get in? I thought they were all railway people here tonight."

"Fisher brought me in, he said you were expecting me." She offered a seductive smile.

"Course I was," said Joe bravely. She attracted him, but she also frightened him. All that rouge, lipstick and confidence made her prominent. But to Joe she looked a bit of a blonde tart, a spider looking for flies and he was nervous about becoming a fly. Yet he couldn't be cold, rejective and dismissive because there might be some excitement for him. He imagined that he liked to live dangerously and she suggested danger so he edged a little closer to the web.

"I haven't seen you lately, Joe, have you been avoiding me?" she muttered seductively.

"I saw you only last Saturday in Beanland's amusements."

"Yes but so did about a dozen others."

"I can't help it if your popular."

"For a fireman Joe, you haven't much fire in your belly."

"Give me a try, You'd find some fire."

"For now Joe just put some fire on the end of this," said Linda placing a Players cigarette between her conspicuous lips.

The evening drifted on amicably enough. Joe hadn't imbibed enough alcohol to be ready to accept Linda's regular invitations to "Come and dance," but gradually he became more inebriated.

"You'll lose her. Get on the floor with her. Get your arms around her," urged Frank Sutton. "When you feel her tits agin yuh chest you'll dance like Fred Astaire," Frank was quite willing to push Joe spider into the web and watch the feast with glee.

"Get me another beer Frank and then I'll go on. I'm only waiting for a really diffi - dificul - difficult dance to come on," slurred Joe exhibiting a tendency to wobble.

"Sit down Joe, before you fall down."

"Get him in the kitchen before he's sick. There's a little bog in there."

"Here drink this." A whisky was poured between his protesting lips. Ready helpers were on hand. Before he could reach out for the bottle Frank had placed on the table he was bodily transported to the small kitchen in the corner and locked in with the bottle by two grinning cleaners planning some kind of sport. Joe's mates, Johnny and Frank knew it was a set up. They just grinned like the little plotting circle of shed men and watched the fuss developing around Linda. She was the star attraction of a little band of conspirators, being plied with drinks and humour and questioned, "Where's Joe? He's been looking for you. He wants to see you Linda."

"He's in the kitchen. He was asking for you Linda." She didn't resist the gentle pressure urging her into the kitchen, she didn't protest when she was pushed through the partly open door and locked in with Joe.

★ ★ ★ ★ ★ ★

2
BLOWBACK

"You look a mess this morning. Like you've been on the beer and then the tiles."

"You're right Jingo," said Joe. "That's about how I feel."

"Been sewing yuh wild oats as well?"

"Nearly. Not by my design. More Fisher Cooke's."

"Tell me more?"

"Not bloody likely, mind your own business," replied Joe in a tone that hinted the subject was closed. "Tell me what we're doing today? The roster just said light engine York."

"York, then Darlington with three engines. Ours, this one here, in steam, and two dead."

"Darlington Shops eh?"

"Yes, all three going for repairs or reconditioning. We're coming back on the cushions. Time I had a soft job."

"I'm surprised you know the route from York to Darlington, Jingo."

"That's why I'm on this job. I'm the only one at Castlebrough that knows that. I worked there during the first years of the war and I've kept in touch with the road ever since.

The loco in steam was the Castebrough engine 2726 the D49 Hunt class 'Meynell', going in for its periodic reconditioning, with it they had to haul a V2 Green Arrow class that had to have its wheels dropped because it had hot axle boxes and an A6 requiring boiler repairs that could not be done in the shed. Darlington workshops was the place all three would receive the correct attention. Joe and Jingo coupled them and obtained a man to ride guard on the last engine and they were off.

An easy 9am journey to York and then on to Darlington on the East Coast mainline. It was a quiet uneventful journey except for the odd pair of frozen points that had to be released by duty platelayers using scrapers and salt to prevent refreezing, or the signals that froze in position and required investigation and then passage on hand signals.

"Darlington, the birth place and home of railways," Jingo explained, thus revealing a side to Jingo's character that took Joe by surprise. "Here in 1825," said Jingo Johnson. "The first public railway in the world, the Stockton and Darlington Railway, was built and operated by George Stephenson. The locomotive was called 'Locomotion'. It's on display on Darlington Station platform. I'll show it you when we go back home on the cushions."

They talked railways as they found their way onto the inspection pits outside of the Darlington Locomotive Engineering Shops. The mass of strange railway networks, and the forests of signals on gantries held no fears for Joe, he knew that Jingo knew his way through the maze. Jingo took him through the workshops where loco's old and new, large and small, where in different stages of renewal or repair. The ease with which mighty overhead beam cranes lifted boilers or locomotives, and lifts that lowered or raised pairs of driving wheels from locomotives in situ' was a staggering introduction for Joe to industrial engineering power.

"You know the Castlebrough to York line, it'll be one hundred years old this year, nineteen-hundred and forty-five. The L.N.E.R. would have had big celebrations this year if there wasn't a war. Forty-two miles of railway, and bridges, and stations built in twelve months using muscle and horse power. Railways and steam engines are here for ever."

The usually impatient Jingo Johnson, especially in the company of a young fireman, was very forthcoming and instructive to Joe, inspired it seemed by being present at the birth place of railways. "We'll call in to the shed time office and pick up a rail pass and then find the train. The guard's gone off on his own. He'll get home before us." They viewed the old locomotive, 'Locomotion' on display on a plinth on the Darlington Station platform and then caught the next south bound passenger train to York.

The railway staff canteen at York, with its famous meat pies, and other cheap non-rationed food beckoned them as they left the London bound train and the guards van they'd travelled in from Darlington. The guard's van was the closest they got to 'travelling back on the cushions'. Trains packed to standing room capacity were the norm of travel even during the first week of the year.

"I'll have two pies if they'll let me."

"You'll be lucky. One each except when they're left over," said Jingo to Joe.

"You'll be lucky," echoed a female voice from just behind Joe. "You're a long way from Whitby, aren't you?"

Carol? Carol Blanchard. The suggestions leapt to his mind and he spun around on the long simple wooden form. He found himself looking up into Carol's clear smooth face. Her red hair seemed more bronze-like and vivacious than when she was on the locomotive at Whitby or more recently at Castlebrough, her hair style more mature, her uniformed canteen smock clasped her bosom. She looked taller than he thought he remembered, taller than her five feet would imply, she'd not grown he realised, she now wore higher heeled shoes. 'She's more of a woman and less of a girl.' The thought flitted through his mind has his smile greeted her.

"Why should I be lucky if I get two pies?" he asked.

"Because I'm on duty," she replied as cheekily as before when she'd 'stowed away' on his engine through Kettleness Tunnel.

"Surely that's a reason why I should get two pies," stated Joe.

"And why I should get two pies as well," joined in Jingo.

"I'll see," she said with a hint of superiority and power. "What are you doing here in York?"

"Just come in from Darlington. Catching the next train to Castlebrough. We're riding on the cushions," replied Joe.

"I'll be catching the three-ten to Castlebrough. and then taking the four-thirty-five from there to Whitby. I'm going to stay with my aunt for four days." added Carol.

"Two pies and a mug of tea," interrupted Jingo, impatiently placing his money before Joe on the other side of the table.

"That alright Carol? queried Joe.

"You'll have to go to the counter and queue. We can't offer waitress service. But I'll come behind the counter and serve you." She laughed. "Ignore that notice that says, 'One pie only for each customer' Just ask for pies and teas."

At the counter Joe told Carol that the next train to Castlebrough was the three-ten and they would be catching that one also. "Maybe I can see you on the train. In an hour."

"Yes, I'll look for you," she replied. "I can't talk now because we are very busy. I'm leaving early today to go through to Whitby so I've got to do as much work as possible."

With two pies and teas nestling comfortably in their stomachs they left the canteen. Jingo said that he was going to get a pint of beer from a nearby pub. "What about you?" he asked Joe. The thought of beer made Joe baulk. The effects of the New Year's celebrations were still with him.

"I think not. I'll see you on number nine platform at the front end at two-thirty Jingo. That's where the three-ten leaves from."

Carol arrived just after the express stopped in platform nine.

Joe was viewing the V2 locomotive which headed the train, Its nameplate, secured on the side of the smokebox carried the name 'Green Arrow'. "Majestic isn't it? And unusually clean." whispered Carol in Joe's ear. She'd stolen up on him unnoticed for the second time in the day.

"Powerful too. Bet she looked beautiful in her prewar livery," said Joe. "I'd like to fire her."

"Never mind you. I would," added Carol.

They were clear of the engine, looking passively towards the tarpaulin sheeted, shadowy cab. The stooped figure of the fireman could be seen labouring away at the fire, his front half brightly illuminated and his back in deep shadow. In the flash of an eyelid it changed; a sudden lance of flame flashed out of the fire box with a heavy 'whoof' into the cab. The fireman staggered, and half-blown, toppled backwards and struck himself against the iron front of the tender. A sudden rushing of steam at the chimney top told Joe that the driver had put the steam blower on hard to avoid any further flashbacks before he moved to help his mate. Joe jumped aboard without invitation and, with the driver, helped the injured fireman to his feet; the man's face and hands were quite badly burned, skin beginning to blister and peel, eyebrows and frontal hair frizzled, he was only partly conscious, clearly quite shocked.

"Send for a doctor or an ambulance," Joe shouted out to Carol and anyone listening. The call echoed down the gathering ranks of onlookers from which Jingo emerged and climbed into the cab to help. The V2 fireman managed to leave through the narrow cab doorway with assistance and was laid on a four-wheeled station barrow, where with the assistance of two porters he was taken away for treatment.

Jingo and Joe were on the footplate with the shocked driver discussing how it had happened and ascertaining that the shaken driver was alright. The Station Inspector joined them on the footplate, a few moments later a locomotive inspector came aboard. The consensus was that the locomotive was in good order to continue; the blow-back had been caused by the sudden combustion of gas in the fire box when the jet blower was not in strong enough operation. "Do you want to be taken off," asked the Locomotive Inspector of the driver.

"I'm alright. Get me a fireman and I'll go on. I'm alright and my mate will be alright in a week or two."

"We'll get a fireman from the shed," the Locomotive Inspector volunteered.

"We're going to Castlebrough on this train if we can help," added Jingo, "My mate's willing to fire it if you get approval for him from control," offered Jingo without asking Joe.

"What about that son? It'd get the train out on time if you could."

"Yes, I could. And I will if you like," replied Joe.

"I'll approve it. Give me your name and seniority date and I'll see that control and Castlebrough gets to know."

"I'll stay on board too and help if you like," volunteered Jingo, "We've both got travel warrants. Just going back to Castlebrough on the cushions. Train's full though."

Joe stepped back into the cab and looked at his charge. The boiler front stood higher than the engines he worked, in fact the scale of everything exceeded any engine he had ever worked on, even the injector controls seemed higher up the boiler face. He checked around that he could recognise the controls, the driver offered some explanations. Joe couldn't resist an outside detailed inspection of 'his' Green Arrow locomotive. It inspired his emotions, fuelled his imagination and his pride. He walked through the crowds along the length of the black-painted fairly clean locomotive. He cleaned both spectacle windows and conveyed the impression that he was making a last minute inspection before the off.

With the fire prepared and waiting for the signal and the green flag, Joe was in conversation with Carol through the cab doorway. "Do you think I could join you on there?" asked Carol knowing she was asking for the impossible. "We might find that we are starting a fashion."

"That would be a sacking job for certain," answered Joe. "Here in York Station with all the spotlights on us, just after the fireman's been burnt by a flashback and taken to hospital. Can you get a footplate pass from your Pop? Then you could come aboard? I think."

The guard's whistle sounded, the signal controlling the exit from number nine platform fell into clear position. The Green Arrow whistle gave its parting blast, a warning to all, whether on the rails, on the platform or in the signal box, that they were off. "All board's off over Ouse Bridge as well," the tall thin Leeds driver shouted to Joe. "We've got fourteen bogies on so'll you'll have to work, she eats a lot of coal." Jingo nodded agreement in

Joe's direction and occupied the fireman's seat for the whole of the forthcoming journey.

The vertically-hanging steam regulator in the hands of the Leeds driver was pulled open with a heave. The sands were blowing on the rails in front as the six coupled driving wheels urged the long train into forward motion. Joe was pleased to get the chance to fire a V2 loco on an express passenger but he was disappointed not to be seated with Carol. Maybe he'd got the choice he most desired. Even though there were two drivers on board he checked again that all of the boards were in clear position and started to fire carefully. Over the long iron Ouse Bridge they slowly heaved. Joe had never felt such power beneath him. The clopperty, clop of the wheels over the jointed rails speeded up as they entered a length of falling gradient and felt the fourteen bogies coming surging after them. Then on past Clifton, up the long gentle rise to Haxby.

Joe fired, kept his eye on the discolourisation at the roaring chimney top and asked the driver about any controls on the engine that were strange to him. The water injectors worked smoothly, the engine steamed magically, the coal was of good quality, visibility was good, the driver didn't bother him. What a perfect ride. He forgot about his diminishing hangover and the hard cold outside. They would be in Castlebrough on time even though they were heavily loaded. Haxby, Strensal, Barton Hill came and went and yet the boiler pressure stood at 225 pounds per square inch.

"I'll be closing off after Barton Hill so we can coast around the bend at Kirkham Abbey," shouted the driver to Joe by way of saying, 'I won't be needing as much steam.' Joe knew of the 45 mile per hour speed restriction through Kirkham Abbey. He closed his dampers to cool his fire, and his mind went back to that horrendous journey with Bob Laker when he'd thrown his shovel in the firebox and never to this day had he ever confessed that to anyone. He was telling himself a lie. He had described the trip very graphically to his paraplegic friend, to their joint amusement. He didn't count Dan as someone he shared confidences with sometimes and not others, he told him everything whether it was something to applaud or condemn.

Darkness was threatening the sky, the signal lights were emerging from the daylight and beginning to send out little sparkles of twinkling light. Soon it would be blackout time and a velvet canopy, with or without jewelled stars, would conceal the clouds and sky and throw its darkness on the countryside and towns.

They obeyed the whistle board and sounded their approach to the Kirkham signal cabin. Joe looked back in the weakening daylight and caught the wave and smile Carol sent from an open window. He enjoyed the forty-five miles per hour coasting run through Kirkham Abbey and Castle Howard, then the steam run through the curves to Hutton's Ambo and on to Malton. The whistle to attract Malton West signalman stirred his blood and he vibrated with excitement as they ran into Malton platform with its few waiting passengers and shot through without stopping. The blast of displaced air fluttered the papers on the station book stall and fanned waiting passengers fluttering their clothes. How glad he was that the fireman had suffered the blow-back. He chastised himself for the thought and settled for the more acceptable thought that 'it is an ill wind that blows no one any good'.

Carol was looking out. The waves and smiles were exchanged again. "Right away mate. All boards off," shouted Joe even though the driver was looking out at the same side and Jingo was alert. Hauling the fourteen coaches up to the maximum war-time 60mph restriction was a tough job even for the powerful Green Arrow but Joe worked hard and enthusiastically and thrilled as they screamed through stations in the developing blackness, whistled for distant signals, and felt the wind of bridges. Castlebrough was waiting, waiting for Joe, or that's how he interpreted every greeting wave from the waiting passengers on number one platform at Castlebrough.

He uncoupled his V2 locomotive, and while they waited for the station shunting pilot to draw their train he enjoyed a relaxed chat with Carol. She had to catch the crowded Whitby and Middlesbrough train at four-thirty- five. She cheered him with the possible news that she may be coming to live in Castlebrough. When he pulled in to the loco shed yard in the darkness with his green arrow he received news which deflated his ballooning spirit.

★★★★★★

3
NOT SO HOT

"Mr Franker wants to see you in his office now. About last night. What did you do to that lass you were in the kitchen with?"

"Nothing. What the hell are you talking about," Joe sounded desperate. He'd never known Bill Clarke to speak so sharply, and without any hint of amusement.

"She was taken to hospital. Unconscious she was. And they said you was involved."

The quick walk up the loco shed yard to the shed master's office was the longest journey he'd ever undertaken. The top roundhouse shed which contained the office seemed blacker and more threatening than usual with its two dim gaslights burning. 'Fancy, Franker being in his office at this time of night. Must be urgent, he never works late unless there's an emergency'. The lights burned in his corner office, he was at 'home', so were others as the sound of voices conveyed. Joe burst in, he was pleased to see there were no strangers there, just Franker in the company of Fisher Cooke, Beilby and Minster, the cleaners who had been so set on introducing Joe to Linda Bakewell.

"What the hell part did you play in that shameful episode last night? Last time I'll attend a shed do. That lass could be dead now." Franker was angry, he wore his trilby hat in the office all the time but tonight he wore his coat and scarf also, it was also a sign that he wasn't on regular duty. He'd come in just to ask questions about what had happened at the New Year's do.

Breath came in short gasps to Joe, with difficulty he responded, "Could be dead?" The visions of removing the dead man from the bottom of the bank at Bempton, the inquest he'd attended about the man and his dead wife came back with an intensity they had not possessed at the time. He filled with a panic he'd not known previously.

"You were with her in the kitchen. She was unconscious. You were gone. I've had her panel doctor on to me. Her parents blamed the railway. As if I'm responsible for a motley crowd of bloody engine cleaners." He would liked to have sworn violently but he was trying to control his temper and his tongue. Cooke and the other two had lost all signs of rebellion, they were cowed, answering only when spoken to.

"I wasn't with her anywhere. I'd only talked to her, not even danced."

"You were in the kitchen with her."

"I wasn't. What's wrong with her? Is she alright now?"

"She should be. But only just. She's been nearly poisoned with alcohol. It can kill you if you get too much. Her Father's been down to see me, for your bloody names." His hand and arm swept in a condemning arc.

"I wasn't with her in the kitchen. When they locked me in the kitchen I let myself out through the back door. I knew where the key was kept. I used it and then hid it in the yard under a brick. Everybody thinks you can't get out of that door 'cos it's locked and not used. I know this place well."

"Why? Why did you go?"

"I knew they were setting me up to get drunk and then plant me in the kitchen and then persuade Linda to come in the kitchen with me for fifteen minutes. Frank told me what they were after so I pretended to be more drunk than I was. They must have put Linda in there without seeing that I'd gone"

"She was in there with you for ten minutes before we opened up to let you out. She was dead drunk then. We thought you'd been let out unnoticed and left her in that state." Fisher tried feebly to prove that someone else was responsible for locking her up in a drunken state.

"You were trying to fix Wade up. That's it, you think everybody's got same stupid bloody mucky minds that you have." Franker walked about irritably. "I can't do anything about the way you 'men' behave. I'd sort some of you buggers out and give you your marching orders if there wasn't a war on."

Franker slammed his hand down on a book on the cast iron fireplace mantle shelf. They jumped. "Get your hands in your pockets. All of you, I'll have two an' a tanner off each of you and go and see her parents with a present from you all."

As they filed out of the office into the darkened shed he had another message. "And you Cooke. A bit less bullying and pranks in the shed. I can get rid of you if I have to." Joe left with the silent group, but drifted from them in the darkened yard without a word and climbed up the steps to the coal stage and Alan Harker.

He confided into the sympathetic ear. "Alan, I feel as though I'm being blamed for getting that young lass drunk. In hospital, with suspected alcoholic poisoning. She's no rough nosed tart. A flirt maybe. I feel grim about it."

"You know who she is don't you?" responded Alan.

"Don't really know who she is? We talk when we meet. She's very friendly, supposed to like me. She's a bit on the young side for me, nearly sixteen, I'm not into the kidnapping game."

"God. You're only seventeen."

"But she's still at school, at the Convent Girls' School."

"She's Tom Bakewell's daughter. He's the Chief Clerk on Goods Outwards side at Gallows Close offices."

"Oh! a railwayman."

"Yes, that's how he's leaned on Franker."

"I'll go and see him. See how his daughter is. Do you know where he lives?" asked Joe.

"On Candler Street, two doors up from Sid Rillington, thirty-three I think. Get Sid's number off Bill Clarke."

"I know Sid's house. I'm going to visit Tom Bakewell when I'm washed up and had some grub."

It was seven o'clock when a suitably scrubbed and brylcreamed Joe nervously knocked on Tom Bakewell's front door. Mrs Bakewell patiently received his stammered request for knowledge of Linda's well being. "Better come in, then I can close the door, got to be careful with the blackout on."

Tom Bakewell was in the comfortable front room listening to the radio. He expressed none of the hostility towards Joe that was expected, he signalled a seat for Joe with the stem of his pipe after the visitor's name had been announced by Mrs Bakewell.

"She's home now. Going to be alright. Mr Franker's had a word with me about you."

He acknowledged Joe's, "Sorry."

"Yes, I know you aren't to blame. How old are you? Linda's only just turned fifteen. She's suddenly growing up. Wants steadying. You are her latest hero. She read about you finding John Cooper. Took the day off school to go and see you at the inquest. She likes you. Doesn't realise you're nearly a man and she's just a little schoolgirl. Come and see her."

She looked pale and ill, reclining in a dressing gown on a chaise lounge in the back room. Joe asked how she was, as politely and as well spoken as he could muster. He could tell that she was pleased to see him, her spirits brightened and her eyes came alive. Her image was totally changed, rouge and lipstick were missing, she looked the part of the sick schoolgirl, Joe bored her for a while with talk about her school, then about his school, then about Dan

West and about Carmel at Snainton. She asked him about his spots. "Had he tried drinking cabbage water." The conversation faltered, even got around to the complexity of the patterns on the embossed ceiling and then Tom Bakewell looked in and asked how she was feeling. "Just tired, and sick, I've been sick a lot today" she added. "Don't know what was in that orange juice I was drinking." That had been her only reference to the previous night.

"I'll have to go now," said Joe shyly. "Maybe you'll get some rest and be better tomorrow."

"She will," said Mr Bakewell as he opened the door and showed Joe down the passage and out through the front door. "Thanks for coming. I know you've been a great help." Almost hinting that he knew something that Joe didn't know. The evening air cooled the excessive sweat on Joe's brow. He wiped it away and blew almost silently through his lips. 'Bloody hell things never go the way you think they're going to go,' he thought. The next day seemed empty. Early morning cleaning shift found him cleaning a loco all by himself, no bullying, no pranks, no relief from the incessant scraping, scratching, and washing of engine parts. Time for thoughts, for plans, for philosophy, time for worrying. There was nothing special to do this afternoon so he pledged to obtain a travel privilege ticket and go out to Snainton on the three o'clock British Queen and have a spirit raising chat with Carmel.

His plans altered when he signed off duty at two o'clock. Bill Clarke gave him a postal delivery letter; white envelope, clear unfamiliar hand writing addressed to Mr Joe Wade, Castlebrough Motive Power Department, L.N.E.R., Castlebrough. "Becoming a regular mailing point for you aren't we?" was Bill's accompanying remark.

Joe opened the envelope as he left the store and set off to the office for his travel ticket. A New Years Card with an illustration of a green- engined distant train making its way through a snow covered landscape. It carried the handwritten message. 'A little late Joe but still in time to wish you all the best 'steaming' for 1945, Carol'.

"Hey you Joe," a voice called out as Joe absorbed the message on the card. Tom West was waving his arms. "Are you going up to our house to see Danny? He heard from the Queen today. Wants to see you." Tom crossed over the intervening lines and joined Joe. "The letter's from Lady-in-Waiting Lucille White. Says the Queen has considered our Dan's request for help and will be informing him as soon as arrangements can be made. She wants his doctor's name and address." Joe was excited he turned away from his journey and went off homeward to see his friend and share the hope that the letter had created. 'Perhaps,' he mused, '1945 is gonna be a good year.'

THE END